GINNY WILLIAMS

A Change of Heart

HARVEST HOUSE PUBLISHERS
Eugene, Oregon 97402

Scripture quotations in this book are taken from the Holy Bible, New International Version. Copyright © 1973, 1978, 1984 by the International Bible Society. Used by permission of Zondervan Bible Publishers. The "NIV" and "New International Version" trademarks are registered in the United States Patent and Trademark Office by International Bible Society.

A CHANGE OF HEART

Copyright © 1995 by Ginny Williams
Published by Harvest House Publishers
Eugene, Oregon 97402

Library of Congress Cataloging-in-Publication Data

Williams, Ginny, 1957–
    A change of heart / Ginny Williams.
      p. cm. — (The class of 2000 series ; 4)
    Summary: When she makes the school's tennis team and tries to fit in with some teammates who are into the party scene, Julie's faith is put to an almost tragic test.
    ISBN 1-56507-326-6
    [1. Christian life—Fiction.   2. Tennis—Fiction
3. Interpersonal relations—Fiction.   4. Friendship—Fiction.]
I. Title   II. Series: Williams, Ginny, 1957–   Class of 2000 ; bk. 4
P27.W65919Ch 1995   94-48342
[Fic]—dc20   CIP
                                    AC

*For Susan—my forever
friend who gives me lots
of space to ask questions.
Thanks!*

O N E

"**F**ifteen-love." Julie Parker wiped the sweat glistening on her forehead with her white terrycloth wristband, and prepared to serve the tennis ball across the net. Her cute face frowned with concentration and her brown eyes sparkled with excitement. Thick, medium length blond hair was pulled back with a red band that matched the trim on her tennis dress.

"Come on, Julie! Ace Greg this time."

Julie grinned at her boyfriend, Brent Jackson. She raised her racquet behind her shoulder, threw the tennis ball in the air, and leaned into it with a grunt. She knew it was a good one when she hit it. Poised in anticipation of a return, she kept her eyes glued on Greg Adams.

Greg reached valiantly for the fast moving serve, but it skimmed the far corner of the serving block and try as he might he couldn't reach it. He groaned in frustration but smiled at his opponent. "Good serve, Julie. Send me another one of those! I'll be ready next time."

Julie returned his smile but couldn't resist taunting him. "Let's see . . . the score is now thirty-love. Once I ace Kelly then I'll only have to serve one more time to finish this match. Yep. Looks like you'll get another chance!"

Kelly Marshall laughed at her friend's cocky words, but the competitive look on her face and the poised readiness of her body indicated she wouldn't go down without a fight. Her long, coppery hair was pulled back into a pony tail. The sweat on her lightly freckled face indicated it had already been a long battle. Tennis wasn't her sport, but she was giving it all she had. Crouched and resting lightly on the balls of her feet, she waited for Julie's next serve.

"Thirty-love." Julie delivered the next serve with as much speed, but it hit squarely in the center of the serving box.

Kelly was ready for it, and returned it smoothly to the back corner.

The fight was on.

Julie met it with an even backhand that sent it back to Kelly's corner. Kelly returned it to the other corner, but Julie was there to meet it. She sent it flying low over the net. Greg jumped to intercept it at the net and smashed it back at Brent. The play continued until Kelly managed a lob over Brent's head and Julie hit it into the net.

"We may go down, but we'll go down fighting!"

Greg crowed as he exchanged high fives with Kelly. His bright blue eyes, so much like Kelly's, glowed with fun. Tennis whites encased his tall, muscular frame, and the waves in his black hair were tighter because of the heat and sweat.

Brent moved over as Julie changed serving position. His curly brown hair framed dancing brown eyes. He wasn't as tall as Greg, but his well-conditioned body supported his passion for soccer. Tennis wasn't his game either, but he always poured all of himself into whatever he did. His eyes narrowed as he focused on the next point.

The battle continued for another ten minutes, but finally Julie and Brent triumphed over Greg and Kelly. Julie, putting all of her strength and concentration into the last serve, put across another beautiful ace that Kelly could not reach.

Julie raised her racquet in triumph as she yelled, "Game and Set!"

The four friends were laughing and breathless as they moved from the tennis court and made room for the next doubles partners who were waiting their turn. Packing up their gear and wiping their sweaty faces with hand towels, they moved toward the small lounge area in the club.

Julie, Brent, Greg, and Kelly had become fast friends over the last semester. Most of the time the two couples double-dated because they enjoyed being together so much. It was Friday night and they had decided to play tennis at the Kingsport

Racquet Club. The almost new facilities defied the February temperature of 20 degrees. Along with the six indoor tennis courts, there were four racquetball courts, a basketball court, and two whirlpool Jacuzzis. It was a great place to hang out and had become a favorite for them.

Kelly sank down into a chair next to a table in the lounge. "Whew! This stuff is exhausting." Tossing her duffle bag to the side, she reached for a menu. "I feel like I haven't eaten in a year! I went straight to the barn after school. Mandy called me this morning and needed me to take over some classes for her. I didn't have time to eat before Greg picked me up." Smacking her lips she turned her concentration to the menu.

Kelly was horse crazy and everyone knew it. She would rather spend time with her horse than anything in the world. Her boyfriend, Greg, was the same way. They both kept their horses boarded at Porter's Riding Stables and spent many hours riding and having fun together. Kelly also taught beginner and intermediate classes on Saturday to pay the board for her black filly, Crystal.

Greg reached for the menu also as he turned to Julie. "I think I've gotten better at tennis since we all started playing here, but I'll never be able to compete with you! If we weren't playing doubles I don't think my pride would even allow me to get on the other side of the net from you. I don't like humiliation that much."

Julie laughed easily. "Let's hope the tennis coach feels the same way you do. I'm pretty nervous about tryouts next week. A lot of these girls have played both their freshman and sophomore years. Waiting until my junior year is going to make it tougher to get a spot, but I'm going to work hard!"

Brent shrugged. "The coach may not know you now, but you'll get her attention pretty soon, I bet!" His smile was warm as he spoke to his girlfriend. They had been dating for about five months and had already been through a lot. It was hard for Brent to comprehend that it had only been a month-and-a-half since he had tried to kill himself. Life looked so different to him now. Sometimes he couldn't believe he had ever tried to take his life.

"Here's hoping," Julie said and then turned to Kelly. The two had become incredibly close in the last six months. "What are you going to eat?"

Kelly studied the menu for a few more moments and then tossed it down. "I don't know. Nothing looks good to me. My folks were having roast beef and baked potatoes when I left. This stuff just doesn't cut it. I know I'm supposed to be a teenager in love with burgers and fries, but sometimes real food is what I want."

Greg nodded. "I know what you mean."

Julie looked thoughtful for a few moments and then stood. "Don't order yet. I'll be right back."

The threesome looked at each other as she walked off with no further explanation. They were used to their friend's impulsive actions so they just shrugged and chatted while they waited. In just a few minutes she was back.

"Let's go," she said as she reached for her bag.

Seeing that she wasn't going to expound on her cryptic comment, Kelly asked the question for all of them. "Go where?"

"My house. I called my mom. She just finished cooking a huge pot of beef stew. She happens to make the best in the world you know. She's also made corn bread and apple pie. She said there was plenty and we could come invade the house if we wanted to."

Her three friends were already grabbing their bags and heading for the door.

"Say no more, my lady," Brent caroled. "We're right behind you!"

Piling into Greg's car they drove the ten minutes to Julie's house and jumped out. Laughing they ran into the house to escape the bitter cold.

A blast of warmth greeted them as they pushed through the door. All of them loved Julie's house. It wasn't big and it wasn't fancy, but it was full of warmth and love. The spacious family room was always available to them. If they weren't at Kelly's, they could usually be found here. They were welcome at Greg's house, but his three little sisters could sometimes turn the place into a zoo. Sometimes they went to Brent's, but he and his mother were still working out their relationship after his suicide attempt, and it was often kind of tense.

"You people aren't exactly dressed for 20-degree weather," Julie's father observed dryly.

Julie laughed as she glanced down at her bare legs. None of them had bothered to put on their sweat suits when they received the invitation to dinner. They had thrown on coats and run. "We wanted to make sure we didn't miss any of the food. Besides, we were so hot the cold felt good."

"It won't feel good if you're all sick in the next few days!"

Brent grinned at Julie's mom and walked over to put his arm around her. "Thanks for the advice, Mom. We promise not to call for chicken soup when we're all dying in bed."

Mrs. Parker smiled as she swatted him with a spoon. "Make sure you don't. I'll just say I told you so and hang up!" Waving them toward the table she complained good-naturedly, "Put four 16-year-olds together and you're guaranteed nothing but trouble!"

The laughing and bantering continued as the group crowded around the table. In addition to the four of them and Julie's parents, there were her brothers, 14-year-old Chris and 10-year-old Matt.

"Let's ask the blessing."

All of them bowed their heads at Mr. Parker's words.

"Lord, thank you so much for all you give us.

Thanks especially for the fun and fellowship we're going to have around this table tonight. Thanks, too, for the food because I'm starving. Amen."

"Amen!" The chorus rose from everyone around the table as they eagerly waited to fill their bowls with the steaming stew.

Silence reigned as the delicious food was devoured. The stew pot was wiped clean, and every one of the corn muffins consumed before conversation returned. Matt and Chris got up to cut the apple pie while Julie, Kelly, and the boys cleared the table.

"Well! I think I like having all this company. I don't have to do any work at all."

"Not so, Dad," Julie laughed. "We're clearing the table, but you still have to load the dishwasher. It's your night you know."

"I was hoping you wouldn't look at the list," her father groaned.

Julie's friends laughed at his comical expression. All of them thought it was great that he helped with the chores. Julie's mother was working to save money for her kids' college tuition so the whole family split up the work.

Once they were settled with warm Dutch apple pie and ice cream, the conversation turned to Julie's hopes of making the Kingsport High School tennis team.

"How did you play tonight, Julie?" her father asked.

"I did okay, Dad."

"Okay?" Brent blustered. "She played great, Mr. Parker! She aced her serve at least a dozen times and had Greg and Kelly all over the court. If she doesn't make the team, that coach is nuts."

Julie blushed her appreciation.

Mr. Parker laughed. "Maybe you should send Brent in ahead of you as your promotion agent."

Julie's mother broke into the conversation. "I just think it's terrific the season is going to start earlier this year. Having the racquet club to practice in is great. I don't know how much they're having to pay to use it, but designating the first four courts for the tennis team is a good idea."

"That's for sure," Julie said. "Being able to play indoors out of the weather until it gets nice was a major plug in my decision to try out this year. I love to play, but I don't enjoy freezing to death outside."

Just then Matt, who had excused himself from the table, came bounding in the dining room. "It's started!"

He was met by blank looks.

He returned their looks with an exasperated one of his own. "The snow! The snow has started!"

"Snow?!" Julie and her friends exclaimed.

Julie continued. "I didn't even know it was supposed to snow."

It took only a few minutes for everyone to polish off the remainder of their pie. Soon they were out walking in the frigid night. The foursome had put on their sweat suits, and all but Julie had borrowed coats and gloves from her parents to keep warm. She was snug in her own snowgear.

It was a light fluffy snow that probably wouldn't accumulate much, but they didn't want to pass up the chance to go for a walk. They didn't usually get much snow in their North Carolina Piedmont town, but this winter had been unusual. There had been snow at least three times a month since December. Spring wasn't too far away so they knew this might be the last snowfall of the year. As they walked, they talked.

"How are things at home, Brent?" Greg asked.

"Pretty good, I guess. Dad and Allison are getting married on April 15. I'm not excited about it, but I've finally learned that I can't live anyone's life but my own. I'm going to make the best of it. I'm glad I know the Lord so he can help me.

"Mom is handling it better than I thought. We talk a lot more now. She is coming out of her depression. The new job has helped a lot. I guess it's made her feel a lot better about herself because she doesn't have to depend on Dad's support to make it. And I like it better because she always made me ask him for money. Mom is really enjoying church since she's started coming. It seems to have helped her and she's made some new friends.

"I know we all have a long way to go, but at least we're all working on it. Dad and I are going on a camping trip without Allison. He realizes he can't force her down my throat. I'm working at getting along with her, but Dad knows we may never be good friends."

His friends nodded thoughtfully. Brent had indeed come a long way from when he had tried to commit suicide with an overdose just before Christmas. It had only been Greg's quick actions that had saved him.

They walked in silence for a few minutes. Julie was the only one who knew the questions raging in her mind. She and Brent had talked some about his suicide attempt and she had felt better, but the doubts had continued to grow.

"Looks like we might get at least a couple of inches," Kelly observed. "The roads seem to be staying clear though. We shouldn't have any trouble getting to the barn tomorrow, Julie. I'll be by to pick you up around 7 o'clock."

Julie nodded and then said, "Why don't we go inside and play Taboo? It's getting cold out here." She didn't add that she also just wanted to get inside where they could laugh and make noise. She was tired of the quiet and peace. It made her think too much, and she wasn't comfortable with her thoughts lately. Her friends were oblivious to her reasons and eagerly agreed.

Minutes later they were crowded around a card table in front of the fireplace where a cheery fire crackled. Julie popped a huge bowl of popcorn, and Mrs. Parker made a pot of hot chocolate. The rest of the night passed in high spirits.

TWO

"Do you really think anyone will show up for your classes this morning, Kelly?" Julie shivered as she climbed into the warm truck and observed, "Cool truck."

Kelly patted the steering wheel and said, "I think so! Dad just bought it last week. He said if we're going to get a trailer to pull Crystal, we needed a truck bigger than the four-cylinder we had. It's kind of a tank to drive, but I'm getting used to it. Dad made me run it through all kinds of stuff before he said I could drive it on my own. He's even going to teach me how to pull the trailer."

She paused and then answered Julie's first question. "And yes, there will be people at class this morning. It's amazing what you'll ride in when you only have one chance a week. There's only a couple of inches of snow on the ground, and the weatherman is predicting temperatures in the 40s today. It will be gone by lunch. If the sun comes out like he said it won't be too bad."

"Okay . . . if you say so. If I were those people I would take one look out the window and crawl back under the covers. That's exactly what I wanted to do. But a promise is a promise."

"And I am so grateful, oh noble one," Kelly laughed. "You know you're dying to go for a ride this afternoon. A few hours of work will do you good. You can laze around in bed some other Saturday. There are us poor working people who never get to have a lazy Saturday."

Julie felt no sympathy. "Yeah? Well you also have a beautiful black horse to motivate you. If I had something like that waiting for me I wouldn't have trouble getting up either. Who knows what hard-headed creature Granddaddy Porter will put me on today."

Kelly laughed at her friend's expression. "It's not that bad. Granddaddy just wants to give you the experience of riding lots of different horses. Anyway, you don't need to worry. He's going to let you ride Ralph. He's super on the trails and easy to get along with."

Julie smiled with delight. "That's great! I love Ralph. We understand each other. He is willing to run when I want to, but he always lets it be my idea instead of his. And his trot doesn't make me bounce to the sky." She leaned back with a sigh. "I'm feeling better already. Aren't we there yet?"

The sky was still cold and gray when Kelly pulled the truck into the driveway of Porter's Riding

Stables. It had long been her favorite place in the
world, and in the six months since Julie had been
coming with her it had become Julie's as well. There
was just something so comforting and peaceful
about the immaculate barns and pastures. This
morning the muted grays of the weathered wood
blended with the sky and painted a mural before
them. Kelly wheeled into the parking lot. As soon
as they stepped out of the truck they were met with
a chorus of whinnies.

Julie laughed. "They seem to know we're the
feeding crew this morning. Mandy must have told
them she was going out of town. Where is she, anyway?"

Kelly moved toward the barn as she talked. "She
went to check on some new class horses for
Granddaddy. It's quite an honor that he asked her.
He used to only go himself. He thinks she's the best
trainer in the state though, so he's letting her do it.
I hope she comes back with some good horses."

Flipping on the lights she moved down the aisle
toward her black filly's stall. She laughed as Crystal
poked her head over the side and snorted as if to tell
her to hurry. Even with her thick winter fur,
Crystal was a beautiful horse.

Some of the owners at the stable kept their
horses in stalls all day with blankets on so that they
wouldn't develop the thick covering, but Kelly
couldn't stand the idea of keeping Crystal confined.
Her filly had grown up wild on the plains of Texas.

The beautiful horse loved to run and play, especially in the snow. She was kept in at night and allowed out to run the rest of the day. Kelly slipped her the carrots she was nosing her pockets for, hugged her neck, and then turned toward the feed room. There was a lot of work to do.

Julie had been roaming around the barn while the morning ritual was taking place. She loved the warmth and coziness. It was always clean and organized, and the horses were given excellent care. She was talking quietly to Ralph when Kelly called her over. Patting his nose she walked over to join her friend. "Okay, slave driver. I am reporting for duty."

The next hour was full of hard work as they shoveled grain and then fed the 40 horses housed in the barn. After they had their grain, hay was taken around and water buckets filled. Julie didn't mind the work. She wasn't as crazy about horses as Kelly, but she had a deep love for them and hoped one day to own her own. She knew how lucky she was to be able to come out and ride with Kelly. Her parents were working hard to support their family and save money for college. There was no extra money for stuff like this. Their one extravagance was the family membership her father had bought at the racquet club.

After feeding and watering all the horses, they grabbed brushes and groomed the 15 that would be used for classes that morning. Once Kelly was satisfied with the job they had done she headed toward the tack room to get saddles.

"Need something hot in your stomachs, girls?"

Julie turned with pleasure at the sound of Granddaddy Porter's voice. "Hi, Granddaddy." She, along with everyone else at the stables, had no relation to the kindly, old man, but he was known by Granddaddy. Julie had no idea what his real first name was.

"Hello, Julie. Good morning, Kelly. I brought you some blueberry muffins that one of my students gave me yesterday. Are you interested?"

"Interested?," Julie exclaimed. "I'm *starving!* I'm glad to know someone thinks about feeding the slave labor around here. Kelly can't think of anything but work."

Kelly rolled her eyes toward her friend. "Can I help it if you're a lazy martyr?"

"Lazy!?" Julie squealed. "I might confess to being a martyr but never to being lazy!" She reached for the plate of muffins. "I'll take those, Granddaddy. I think Kelly is too interested in her work. I'd hate to influence her into becoming lazy like me. I'm sure she's not hungry."

It was Kelly's turn to squeal and dive for the plate of muffins. Granddaddy just laughed. "Enjoy them. When you're done you can come in for something to drink." He looked around the barn with contentment. "I love being in here when the horses are eating. There's just something special about the sound of their munching."

Julie nodded as she stuffed a muffin in her mouth. "Right now I'm more interested in my munching."

Kelly shook her head. "She's hopeless, Granddaddy. Greg says all I think about is food. I'm nothing compared to her!"

"Not true," Julie protested around a full mouth. "I've been working hard all morning. I deserve some nourishment to keep me going."

Granddaddy Porter laughed again and walked from the barn. It took the girls only a few minutes to demolish the muffins. Then they turned back to their labor. In another 30 minutes they had all the horses saddled, bridled, and tied to their places in the barn aisle.

Kelly glanced at her watch. "Thanks, Julie. We made good time this morning. We still have 20 minutes before the first student comes. Let's go over to the house and get something to drink."

Both girls downed large glasses of cold milk and had another muffin before they saw the first car pull in.

The morning passed in a flash as Kelly taught all the intermediate and advanced classes, and Julie handled the beginners. Julie was thrilled that Granddaddy trusted her enough to let her teach. She knew that she must really be improving or he wouldn't have allowed her to do it. She was pleased, but her passion was her tennis. She could only hope she was good enough to make the team. She would know by the end of next week.

• • •

Julie pulled the bridle onto Ralph's head, adjusted the bit to make sure it was comfortable, and mounted. Kelly, already on Crystal, was waiting impatiently.

Julie grinned at her friend. "Let's go!" This was always her favorite part of helping Kelly. Her friend knew all the trails around the barn and they had had hours of fun exploring them together. Today there was the added bonus of the lingering snow. Hazy sunshine peeked through wispy clouds to dissipate the dull gray of the morning sky.

As the girls entered the woods, they became quiet and enjoyed the sanctuary. Julie, looking around, saw the first signs of spring. Tiny green buds on the end of the maple branches seemed to whisper that soon they would be released from the spell of winter and break into the glory of a new season. Even with a chill still dominating the air, there was a hint of softness promising the approach of warmth and new life.

Julie took a deep breath and shivered with delight. She reached down and gave Ralph a big hug. As she leaned against his solidness she sensed the change come over him. Without looking, she knew they must be about to reach the opening into the pasture. Straightening, her eyes confirmed what she already knew.

Julie was ready when Kelly whooped and lunged forward onto Crystal's neck. She knew Ralph was no match for Crystal's speed, but he was fast and she loved to run with him through the fields. Taking a tighter grip with her legs, she gave the large gelding his head and urged him forward. He had waited for her signal but had been shaking his head impatiently. Kelly and Crystal were already halfway across the field before Ralph raced after them. That suited Julie just fine. It wasn't a race. It was just a run for the fun of it.

Two hours later they turned back down the same trail they had started on. Both girls and horses were tired but content from the fun and exercise. They were quite happy just to amble through the woods and let the peace wrap around them.

Kelly's next words shattered Julie's peace.

"Brent seems to be doing really well. I'm glad things are going so well with his folks."

Julie nodded, but once more her thoughts were in turmoil. She said nothing.

Kelly looked carefully at her friend. "Are you okay, Julie?"

Julie said yes, but avoided looking into her friend's eyes. She knew she didn't lie very well.

Kelly paused and then asked, "What are you thinking?"

How Julie hated that question sometimes! Their youth director, Martin Stokes, had taught them to ask it when they were helping Brent learn to talk and work through his feelings. She wanted to scream that it was none of Kelly's business, but she didn't want to hurt her. She wanted to lie and say she wasn't thinking anything, but the truth was that she was getting tired of carrying the burden of her questions alone.

"I guess I still struggle with Brent's suicide attempt." Only she knew how much of an understatement that was.

"In what way?" Kelly asked.

Julie struggled to express herself. "I think I can understand why he felt the way he did. But it made me angry after I got over feeling so guilty. I've stopped being angry, but now I have so many questions."

She paused for so long that Kelly pressed her again. "What kind of questions?"

Julie plunged ahead. "Questions like how God could allow things to get so bad in his life that he would want to kill himself. Questions like why God didn't stop him from taking all those pills. Questions like why he almost died." The words seemed to pour from her lips. She hesitated and then blurted out the real question that had been eating her for the last month-and-a-half. "Questions like I wonder if God really exists! And if he does, does he really have anything to do with our lives and how we live!"

Silence filled the woods after her desperate words. She could tell by the look on Kelly's face that she had shocked her, but Julie was grateful that she wasn't jumping in and trying to provide her with answers. They rode quietly for a few minutes before Kelly spoke.

"I don't know what to say, Julie. Of course you know I believe God exists. I haven't been a Christian for long, but God is very real to me. I sure don't know how to prove it to you , though. I had no idea you were thinking about these kinds of things."

Julie shrugged her shoulders. "I try not to, but I can't help it. I mean, I've grown up in a Christian family. A great family! I've prayed to God for as long as I can remember, and I can't think of a time I didn't know he was there and cared about me. But it seems lately I'm having a hard time believing all that any more." Julie could tell Kelly just didn't know what to say.

"Thanks for not preaching at me. I don't expect you to have any answers. This is something I'll just have to figure out on my own. I'll be okay!" Her bright words were spoken to cover the heaviness in her heart. "Let's get back to the barn. I'm starving again. I bet Peggy has a great dinner for us!" She urged Ralph into a trot and headed down the trail.

Kelly allowed Crystal to break into a trot also, but gazed after her friend thoughtfully. She'd had no idea Julie was grappling with these questions. All of them had been shocked when Brent tried to kill himself, but his relationship with the Lord was good again and so much was changing in his life. Kelly had been excited about the evidence of God at work. She had no idea how to help her friend.

● ● ●

By the time Julie got to Kelly's house she had managed to shake off her somber mood. She loved going there. Peggy, Kelly's stepmother, was a terrific cook and a lot of fun. Kelly's father always made Julie feel welcome and like she was part of the family. Even Emily, Kelly's 12-year-old sister, was great to be around.

It was 5:30 P.M. and almost dark when they pushed the door open and walked into the kitchen. Julie's eyes sparkled with delight when she saw the fixings for tacos lining the kitchen counter. She rubbed her stomach in anticipation.

"I take that as a symbol of hunger." Peggy smiled at the girls from where she was standing at the sink. "Long day?"

Kelly and Julie sank down on the stools next to the counter and reached for some tortilla chips. Kelly's mouth was full so Julie spoke. "Not too bad. Everything ran smoothly but we are definitely starving."

Peggy nodded. "We'll be ready to eat in a few minutes. Emily went skating with some friends. She should be here any minute."

As if beckoned by Peggy's words, Emily walked through the kitchen door and headed straight to the chip bowl. Peggy intercepted her and reached for the bowl just as Kelly moved to get more.

"That's enough you three! There won't be any for dinner if you keep munching. Go wash up and call your father. Then we can get down to some serious eating."

It didn't take long to devour dinner. Then Julie headed upstairs with Kelly to change before Greg and Brent came over for the evening.

"Do you know what the guys have planned for tonight?" Julie asked. A month or so ago they had decided to alternate planning dates. She and Kelly planned one weekend, the guys planned the next. That way the guys didn't always have to come up with new things to do. And whoever planned it had to pay for it. The new method had worked great so far. Julie had learned a lot more appreciation for the money the guys spent on them, and they had fun trying to come up with inexpensive things to do.

"I have no idea," Kelly responded. "Last night was a money night for everyone but you, since you have a membership at the club, so it will probably be something that won't cost much. Usually they tell us if we need to wear something special. They haven't said anything so I'm going for a clean pair of jeans and a sweater."

"Good. That's what I brought with me. I'll flip you for the shower."

The resulting heads gave Julie the hot shower first. They were both ready when the boys knocked on the kitchen door and came in.

Julie knew she looked good that night. Her medium length blond hair was waved gently away from her face and the day's exercise had given a glow to her face. Her green sweater brought out the flecks of green in her brown eyes. She was tired but ready for some fun.

Brent's eyes told her he agreed with her evaluation of her appearance. He looked pretty good himself in his red sweater and black jeans.

Greg waved everyone to places around the table. "Okay girls. Here's the plan for the night." He paused dramatically. "We're going ballroom dancing."

"Excuse me. Would you repeat that please?"

Greg grinned at Kelly. "I said we're going ballroom dancing."

Kelly and Julie stared at each other and then at their dates.

Julie spoke next. "What in the world are you talking about? Where are we going dancing? What am I talking about?! Forget *where*. We don't even know *how* to ballroom dance!"

"Exactly!"

The girls waited for Brent to expound on his single word, but he wasn't adding anything.

Kelly saw Peggy grinning at the two boys. "Okay. That's enough! Cut the riddles. What in the world are you talking about?" Then she turned to Peggy. "And what do you know about this?"

Peggy grinned again, but disappeared through the door into the family room.

Kelly spun around to stare at Greg.

Greg laughed. "Okay, here's the scoop little miss spit-fire. Brent and I got some free lessons for ballroom dancing."

"Yeah," Brent chimed in. "We thought it would be fun to try something new and it won't cost us anything. Actually, Kelly, Peggy told us about the lessons. She and your Dad did it last year and said they had a blast. Greg and I thought it was crazy at first because we don't know the first thing about it. Then we decided that if all we do is spend the evening laughing at each other we'll still have fun and it won't cost us anything!"

By now Julie and Kelly were laughing at Brent's theatrical defense of their plan. Exchanging glances they shrugged in defeat.

"Whatever you say," Julie laughed. "We probably *will* spend all night laughing at each other, but it does sound like fun. At least it will be something different!"

The boys exchanged relieved looks. They hadn't been at all sure the girls would go for the idea.

• • •

The evening passed in a flash as they stumbled across the dance floor in an imitation of the waltz. Julie had thought she would melt with embarrassment until she realized the other couples were having just as much trouble as she and Brent were. They weren't watching her. They were trying to learn themselves. Once she relaxed and quit being so self-conscious, she began to enjoy herself. By the end of the two hours she and Brent were giving a passable performance of gliding across the floor. She had never danced like this before, but she had to admit she was having a great time. A quick glance around the room told her Kelly and Greg were having fun, too.

The music for the last song ended. Yet as the foursome left the dance floor, the tune started up again. The lights dimmed, and an elegantly dressed couple glided into sight. They dipped and swayed as they waltzed gracefully across the floor. After a few moments the music switched and they broke into a lively rendition of the Charleston. The music switched again and they were doing the Rhumba. As the music flowed from one short snatch of a song to another the couple changed their dance steps as they laughed into each other's eyes.

Julie and Kelly caught their breath in appreciation. Even the boys seemed to be impressed.

The music ended and their teacher stepped forward. "That is a demonstration of what 12 weeks in this class will teach you. Any of you who are interested in taking the full course can talk to me now. Thanks all of you for coming."

The four friends laughed and talked all the way home. Someday Julie wanted to learn to dance that way, but it wouldn't be anytime soon. Four hundred dollars was just a little out of her reach.

"Brent, that was a great idea. I had a lot of fun. Thanks."

"I'm glad, Julie. We weren't sure whether you would think we were crazy or not, but we decided to go for it."

"I'm glad you did," Kelly said. "We're going to

have a hard time topping this next week. I'm going to have to check out some books on dates from the library. Maybe we'll get some ideas that way!"

"If you have any trouble, we might take pity on you and help."

Kelly stuck out her tongue at the sound of Greg's self-righteous tone. "We won't need any help from you, big guy. Just be ready for some fun!"

"Ahhhhh. I knew the competitive spirit would take over if I played with your pride a little bit!"

Kelly could do nothing but laugh at the satisfied look on his handsome face. She knew she had walked right into his trap.

Just then Greg drove up in front of Julie's house and Brent jumped out to walk her to the door.

"Thanks a lot, Brent. I really had a great time."

Brent smiled and leaned forward to give her a soft kiss. "I'm glad. See you tomorrow at church."

Julie leaned against the door once she had walked into the house. Her life was really going so well. Why did she have to have all these annoying questions? And even though she'd had a terrific time with Brent tonight, things just didn't seem to be the same between them. What was going on with her?

THREE

J ulie twirled her racquet nervously as she waited for Mrs. Crompton, the tennis coach, to call all of them together. The first day of tryouts was finally here. She would give it her best, but she had no idea if she could compete against these other girls. As she waited, Julie eyed the group.

There were 24 girls gathered at the racquet club, all dressed in tennis whites. Some wore shorts, some were in dresses. Racquets ran from the very expensive to the more basic ones. Julie recognized a few of the girls, but there was no one she knew well. A couple of the girls went to the church across town that her youth group had done some things with, but all she knew about them were their names. She made no effort to go greet them. For some reason she didn't want to connect herself to other Christians at the very beginning.

Just then the very two girls she was thinking about noticed her and walked over.

"Hi, Julie! Do you remember us?"

Julie pushed aside her thoughts and met them with a bright smile. "Of course, Becky!" She made room beside her for the tall blond. "And you're Susan, right?" There was just room on the other side for the petite brunette to squeeze in.

"You have a great memory," Becky said. "We only saw each other once last fall when we did that retreat together. How are things going in your youth group?"

Julie smiled, but she was thinking furiously how she could get out of this conversation. She didn't want to talk about church things. From what she could remember, both of these girls were leaders in their church and were probably committed Christians. She forced a cheerful note in her voice. "Oh, great! We're going on our Spring Retreat next weekend. We're going skiing up at Wintergreen Ski Resort." Julie noticed that several other girls were listening to their conversation. Just then Mrs. Crompton saved her from having to talk about any more church stuff.

"Okay, girls. Let's all find a seat on the benches. We have some things to talk about."

Julie breathed a sigh of relief as silence fell on the group. She was here to play tennis. That's all she wanted to think about just then.

"It's good to see all of you here. My list says there are 25 of you. My count says the same thing. I won't remember all your names for a while, but I want to at least start connecting faces. I'm going to call your names. Just let me know who you are."

Julie paid close attention as she called out the
names. She especially wanted to know the names of
the three girls who had been listening as she talked
with Becky and Susan. The muscular girl, who at
5'7" was the same height as she, was Sandy. The
pretty redhead with the perfect smile was Carla.
The cute brunette with the short hair and serious
eyes was Jennifer.

Mrs. Crompton put down her list as she read the
last name. "Okay, everyone is accounted for. We
have a lot of work to do this week so I'm going to
talk as little as possible. I'm here to watch you play
tennis. I wish all of you could make the team, but
that's just not possible. There will be two cuts. One
on Wednesday and the final one on Friday. The
final number will be 11 girls. How you play is
important, of course. Just as important to me is
your attitude and your team spirit. Kingsport High
has always had a good tennis team. I have great
hopes for this year as well. We'll talk more about
things as we go along. Any questions?"

Scanning the group, she was met with silence.
"Okay, then let's get started. We only have four
courts so I'm going to put six of you on each one.
The first two names I call on your court will practice for ten minutes, and then switch with the next
two until everyone has had a chance to warm up.
Then we'll do some drills." Looking at her list she
called out names for each court.

Julie didn't hear her name until court number

four was called. She was grouped with Becky, Carla, Sandy, Jennifer, and a girl named Blair. The group eyed each other nervously. Who would make the team and who wouldn't? Julie noticed that the only two who didn't seem nervous were Carla and Sandy. They had an air of confidence that bordered on cockiness. It didn't take long to find out why.

"Let's go, Carla. Our names were called first." Sandy picked up some balls and moved to the far side of the court.

Within minutes the two were smoothly volleying the ball back and forth across the court. Julie watched as they sent shots deep into the corners and then raced to intercept them at the net.

"They're good, huh?"

Julie turned to see who was speaking. "You're Jennifer, aren't you?" she asked.

"Yeah. What's your name again?"

"I'm Julie."

"Hi, Julie. Is this your first time trying out?"

"Yeah." Julie couldn't keep her eyes off the two playing. She would have to play great tennis to be able to compete with them.

Jennifer noticed her intense scrutiny of the pair. "That's Carla and Sandy."

Julie didn't bother to tell her she knew their names already.

"They were number one and two seed on the team last year. They've played all through high school. They're both seniors."

"They're good!"

"Yeah. They're good and they both know it. But they're both nice enough. We're not great friends, but we party together on the weekends."

Julie glanced at Jennifer again but didn't say anything.

"You go to parties much?" Jennifer asked.

"No, that's not really my scene," Julie shrugged casually.

"Yeah. I heard you and those other two talking. Sounds like you're pretty much into the church scene."

Julie paused and thought before she answered. She knew this was a great opportunity to invite Jennifer to church. In the past she would have done that. She had gotten a lot of her friends to start going to church. But that was before all the questions about God had started coming into her mind. Now she didn't know where she fit.

"Oh, it's okay. It's not really that big of a deal."

Jennifer looked at her closely but didn't say anything else.

Julie tried to ignore the knot in her stomach. She was here to play tennis, not to try and tell people about a Jesus she wasn't even sure existed. She watched Sandy and Carla for a few more minutes before the coach's whistle signified a change.

"Looks like it's our turn, Julie."

Julie looked at Jennifer in surprise. "Are we playing together? I guess I wasn't listening to the list very well. I haven't even asked you. Have you played on the team before?"

"The last two years. Last year I was number six on the team. I'm not all that great, but I love to play so I guess that makes up for it."

Julie laughed along with her. She already liked Jennifer. She might be a "partier," but there was something about her that was really appealing. Maybe it was the combination of her gentle smile and serious eyes.

Taking the court, Julie hit the ball into the net a few times before she was able to relax. She was here to play tennis. That was all. If she didn't make the team it wouldn't be the end of the world. Once she settled down, her shots flew low and hard across the net. She forced Jennifer all over the court in pursuit of her returns. She could hardly believe ten minutes had passed when the whistle blew again for a change. Mopping her face she followed Jennifer from the court.

"Where have you *been* for the last two years? You can flat out play some tennis!"

Julie laughed at the admiration in Jennifer's voice. "Thanks, Jennifer. I just get out there and have fun. I've been busy with other things the last couple of years so I didn't try out for the team."

"Things like your church stuff?"

Julie turned at the sarcastic words thrown her way. "What?" she asked in confusion.

Carla laughed mockingly as she pushed her flowing red hair back from her face and clipped it. "I said you must have been busy with all your church stuff. Is that what kept you from playing tennis?"

Julie's mind raced. She didn't want to make enemies on the first day and besides she didn't really feel like defending church right now. She decided to ignore the sarcasm. "No, church isn't that big of a deal to me. I've been singing in the school choir and that took a lot of time. I just decided I wanted to try and play tennis this spring."

Carla shrugged her slender shoulders and turned away to talk with Sandy.

Julie sat down and tried to concentrate on Becky and Blair playing. Why was Carla treating her like that? She surely hadn't done anything to her.

"Don't worry about Carla. She doesn't like competition. She recognizes talent when she sees it," Jennifer said.

Julie protested, "I'm not as good as she is!"

"Don't be too sure. I've played Carla, and now I've played you. I bet you could beat her. Anyway, she's not much on the church scene. But then, neither am I."

Julie shrugged. "I'm just here to play tennis."

Jennifer nodded. "That's what I'm here for, too. Let's go. I think Mrs. Crompton is getting ready to call us together for drills."

Julie watched the other courts as she strolled over to the meeting area. There were some other good players, but she was pretty sure she could play as well as them. Playing Jennifer had helped her confidence a lot. Jennifer had been on the team last year. Julie knew she could beat her if they played. She wasn't sure she could handle Carla or Sandy, but she didn't have to be able to beat the top two players. She just had to be one of the top 11. She determined to work as hard as she could.

The next hour-and-a-half passed in a flash as Mrs. Crompton ran them through serving drills, net play, backhand and forearm drills, and lots of running. Julie was dripping with sweat when the coach finally called them all back together, but she had had a super time and knew she had done well. She had caught Mrs. Crompton watching her closely several times.

"Okay, girls. Everyone did a good job today. I hate to think of having to cut anyone, but that's the reality of this sport at this school. Not everyone will be a part of the team. Just know from the start that it's going to be a tough decision on my part. If you don't make the team don't feel bad. Just continue enjoying tennis. That's the great thing about this sport. You don't have to have a team to play. You can grab your racquet and one other person and play anytime you want." Smiling at the girls, Mrs. Crompton waved them toward the locker rooms. "The showers are waiting. And if I may be so honest, y'all definitely need them!"

Everyone laughed as they grabbed their stuff and headed toward the ladies' locker room. Julie thought longingly of the Jacuzzi, but knew it was off limits to the team. That hadn't been part of the agreement with the school. Oh well, she could come back later if she wanted to.

"You've got a good chance to make the team, Julie."

"Thanks, Jennifer. I hope so. But even if I don't, I'm having a good time." She turned to smile at her new friend, but the words directed from behind her caused her smile to fade.

"As good a time as you have at *youth group?*"

Julie turned around to stare at Carla. She bit back the hot words that sprang to her lips. What was with this girl? She met her eyes evenly, shrugged, and turned away toward her locker. She didn't want to make enemies before she even made the team. It was for sure Carla and Sandy would be a part of it. She wanted to fit in. She didn't want to be an outcast for something she wasn't even sure she believed any more.

Julie let the hot water pound into her tired body. She couldn't get Carla out of her mind. Then she thought of Jennifer and smiled. If she made the team she would at least have one friend. She thought about Becky and Susan, too. She knew they could be friends but she was just so confused about all the God stuff. She didn't want all of her associations on the team to be Christians until she figured out what she believed. Mentally shaking her mind clear, Julie turned off the shower and quickly dried and dressed. Brent would be here in a few minutes to pick her up.

Julie's spirits rose when she saw Brent waiting for her in the lobby of the club. As she waved goodbye to Jennifer she noticed Carla and Sandy in the corner. They had their heads together and it was obvious they were talking about her. Julie turned away and took Brent's arm. She was determined not to let them bother her.

The sun was setting as Julie and Brent went outside.

"I sure will be glad when spring gets here. I can hardly wait until the days are longer. I have to get up in the dark to get ready for school and now it's going to be dark when I leave practice. I miss the sun!" Julie complained.

"Yeah. I know what you mean. At least it's only another month before it really starts acting like spring. I sure am glad I don't live up north. I've enjoyed the snow this year, but if we still had a couple more months to look forward to, I would be going nuts." Brent rolled his eyes for emphasis.

"You and me, both!" Julie slid into his car and then turned in anticipation. "Didn't you say something about ice cream?"

Brent laughed as he slid behind the wheel. "Hungry?"

"Hungry isn't the word for it. I didn't eat much lunch because I was so nervous. Now I'm starving!"

Brent started his compact car and wheeled out of

the parking lot. "Friendly's Ice Cream coming up. I talked to Greg and Kelly. They're going to meet us there. We decided to celebrate your first day of tryouts with a real meal. Hamburgers and sundaes coming up, my lady!"

Julie laughed but questioned him. "How did you know we would get to celebrate? What if I hadn't done well?"

Brent scoffed. "I know how well you play tennis! Come on, admit it. You did great today, didn't you?"

Julie smiled and then laughed. "Okay, you're right. I did pretty good. I think I have as much a chance as anyone of making the team. I'm going to try my hardest anyway!"

Brent squeezed her hand. "You'll make it. Mrs. Crompton may be a tough coach, but I know her and she's neither blind nor crazy. She won't let you go."

Julie was glowing at his words as they pulled into the parking lot of Friendly's and went inside to join Greg and Kelly. Julie was able to put aside all of her questions and the uncomfortable feelings about Carla and Sandy as they laughed their way through the meal. These were her friends. She would make sense of everything else.

FOUR

J ulie grabbed an extra carton of milk as she walked through the cafeteria line. The grilled chicken sandwich on her tray wouldn't appease her hunger for long, but she just didn't think she could eat anymore. She was too nervous.

"Nervous?" Kelly asked with a smile.

"How did you know?" Julie placed her tray on the table next to Brent's and turned to where Kelly and Greg faced her from the other side of the table. The four of them always sat together at lunch.

Kelly laughed. "That's easy. You have about a fourth of the food you usually put on your tray! Whenever you're not eating I know something is wrong."

Julie nodded. "The final cut is this afternoon."

Brent laughed. "As if we didn't know! That's all you've talked about this week."

Julie instantly looked remorseful and said quickly, "I'm sorry. I've probably driven you all crazy, haven't I?"

"You've done nothing of the kind," Kelly said firmly. "Brent just meant we are all aware of what day it is. We'd all be nervous, too."

Brent and Greg nodded at Kelly's words.

"She's right, Julie. I didn't mean to make you feel bad," Brent said. "I remember how worked up I was when I was trying out for the soccer team. I thought I'd done okay in tryouts but I wasn't at all sure I'd make the team."

Julie felt better at his words. If Brent had been nervous then it was okay for her to be nervous. After all, he was the best soccer player at Kingsport High.

"How's it going with Carla and Sandy?"

Julie frowned at the mention of the two girls. "Oh, I don't know about them. They'll make the team for sure. They haven't talked to me much since Monday. They just kind of ignore me. I had to warmup with Carla yesterday, but she didn't say one word to me. I hear them talking in the locker room, though. There is going to be a big party with a lot of beer somewhere this weekend. They were inviting different people on the team to go. It sounds like they do it all the time."

"Who do they get to buy the beer for them?" Brent asked. "The store clerks in this town are pretty strict about carding kids."

Julie shrugged. "I have no idea. It doesn't seem to be a problem, though."

Greg agreed. "Kids can get alcohol if they want it. There's always someone who will buy it for them.

I've heard some things about Carla and Sandy around school. They hang out with a pretty wild bunch. Sounds like you'll have some good chances to share your faith if you make the team, Julie."

Julie just nodded at Greg's words. She knew that's what she should be thinking, but to tell the truth it hadn't once crossed her mind.

"Yeah, Julie," Brent agreed. "Have you thought about asking any of them to the Ski Retreat?"

Tomorrow morning the youth group was meeting in the church parking lot at 6 o'clock to head out for two days of skiing and meetings. They weren't due back until Sunday night.

Julie shook her head. "I asked a few of them," she lied, "but they couldn't come. I'm sure I'll have plenty of opportunities to tell them about the Lord and ask them to come to church." Julie cringed at her lie, but she just couldn't tell them the truth. She knew how to say all the right words. She could play the game and no one would know all she was struggling with. Looking up she saw Kelly regarding her, but Julie quickly changed the subject.

"Is everything still set for Valentine's Day?" Julie directed the question at the boys because they had insisted they were going to plan everything. It was their week, they said. The girls had insisted it was theirs because the Ski Retreat was making them miss their turn, but the guys said they already had everything under control.

Kelly turned eager eyes toward Greg. Would he

reveal any clues as to their plans? Her hopes were dashed when he merely winked at Brent and shrugged his shoulders.

"I guess you'll have to wait and see, but yes, I'd say things are set. Wouldn't you, Brent?"

"Definitely. I think this may go down as the Valentine's Date of the century."

Julie and Kelly exchanged exasperated looks but knew they would get no more information out of the guys.

Julie decided to reveal the good news she had been holding back. She had wanted to wait until she was sure she had made the team, but she couldn't resist talking about it.

"I did learn something else at practice yesterday." Her voice was deliberately tantalizing. She waited until the other three had their eyes fixed on her and then continued. "I learned about an annual tradition of the tennis team." She paused, smiled, and said, "They spend every Spring Break in Florida."

"Florida?" Kelly squealed. "Julie, that's great. You've always wanted to go there!"

Julie let her smile widen with excitement. "I know! Wouldn't it be great? Florida in March. I'd get a head start on spring and on my tan! Now I just have to make the team."

● ● ●

Julie took a deep breath of the crisp, winter air.

The day was cold but crystal clear, and the sun was shining brightly. After the clouds of the last few days she longed to stay outside and enjoy the sun, but practice was due to start in just a few minutes. She leaned back against Jennifer's car, soaked up the rays, and tried to get her nervousness under control.

"I don't know why you're nervous," Jennifer said. She had moved around to where Julie was standing. "I've seen Mrs. Crompton watching you. You're definitely going to make the team. I'm the one who should be worrying. You might be getting my spot!"

Julie smiled at her new friend. In the week they had been trying out together they had become closer. Julie didn't really know that much about Jennifer, but she liked her. "We both have to make the team," she said firmly.

"Fine. We'll both make the team. But not unless we show up for the final day of tryouts. If you are through being Miss Nature-child, we can go in and play tennis."

Julie laughed and followed Jennifer into the racquet club. She would do her best and then she would just have to live with the consequences.

Julie gripped her racquet tightly and crouched into a ready position. She could hardly believe she had been slated to play Sandy, and almost groaned out loud when Mrs. Crompton had read their names off the list. Why did she have to play the number one player today? She could only hope Sandy wouldn't

make her look like a rank beginner. Sandy had
merely given her a smug look when she heard who
she was to play and had walked around to her side of
the court without saying anything. Julie still didn't
know why Sandy and Carla disliked her so much,
but she was determined not to let it bother her.

Sandy sent a ball smashing into her court, but
Julie was ready. She returned it low over the net
into the far corner. The battle was on!

At the end of an hour of intense play, Sandy was
leading five games to four. It had been a hard fought
battle, and Julie had caught her opponent studying
her several times as if surprised at having to work so
hard. When Mrs. Crompton blew the whistle neither had won the set. They both knew it could have
gone either way.

"Nice playing."

Julie could only stare after Sandy's back after she
had spoken the two words and walked off. Had she
really said something nice to her?

"She recognizes good playing, anyway."

Julie turned as Jennifer spoke and said, "She's a
great tennis player. I just can't believe she was nice
to me."

"Oh, Sandy's okay. You just have to get to know
her. She can be a lot of fun. Hey, we're going to a
party tonight. You ought to come along. You'll see
a different side of Sandy and Carla. I don't know
what's been bugging them about you, but they'll get
over it. Hanging out together at a party might be

just the thing."

Julie looked at Jennifer. Was she that much into the party scene? She didn't really look the type. But then, what did Julie know about partying? She had been a Christian all her life and had never gotten involved in that stuff. She didn't know what was or wasn't the type. She didn't want to look totally ignorant or show that she had never been to a party like that before.

Julie shook her head. "I can't. Thanks for the invitation but I already have plans."

Jennifer shrugged. "Maybe some other time."

"Yeah," Julie agreed. As they walked over to where Mrs. Crompton was waiting for them she thought about the invitation. Part of her wanted to go and see what it was all about. After all, she wouldn't have to drink. Julie almost laughed at herself. Her friends would freak out if she said she was going to one of those parties. Then her thoughts became more serious.

Was she allowing herself to be controlled by what others thought? If she wasn't even sure God existed anymore, why should her old set of beliefs dictate how she acted now? Why should she miss out on a new kind of fun? Julie shook off her wonderings and sat down next to Jennifer. She couldn't go tonight, that was for sure. She and Kelly already had plans with Brent and Greg. She was sure, though, that the issue would come up again. What would she do next time?

Mrs. Crompton picked up her clipboard and eyed the 18 girls watching her with nervous anticipation. "I'm sure you think I say this every year, but I really don't. I had more trouble this year than any other deciding who would make the final team. I really wish I could keep you all. If you didn't make the team this year please come back and try again next year. We will have several seniors graduating off the team and there will be some spaces for good players. I'm not going to say anything else except to thank you for all your hard work. Now I'll read off the final team names. If you are on the team please go over to court number one for our first team meeting."

She checked her clipboard again and began to read. "Sandy Jones, Carla Gresham . . ."

Julie leaned forward eagerly. She had expected the first two names.

"Amy Johnson, Laura Matthews, Jennifer Patterson . ."

Julie turned to smile at her friend and squeezed her hand in congratulations. Then she turned back to hear the coach's voice.

"Sarah Andrews, Marilla Preston, Jewel Campbell . . ."

There were only three more to go. Would she make the team? Julie held her breath as she waited for the last three names.

"Francis Laird, Amanda Fields and last, but not least, Julie Parker!"

Julie leaned back with a huge sigh of relief. She had made it!

"I told you we would be playing together!"

Julie turned to Jennifer with a wide smile and impulsively hugged her. "I should have listened to you all along! I can't believe I actually made it!"

Jennifer laughed at her excitement. "You not only made it, but I will go so far as to predict you will be in one of the top three positions soon."

Julie scoffed, "Yeah, right!"

Jennifer just shrugged. "Time will tell. Just remember what I said." Looking over Julie's shoulder, she said, "Let's go. You don't want to be late for your first official team meeting."

Spirits were high in the locker room after the meeting. Mrs. Crompton hadn't kept them long. She had congratulated them all on making the team and encouraged them to have a good weekend. She said they had earned it! Julie couldn't have agreed more.

Jennifer and Julie laughed and talked as they showered and changed clothes. They were joined in their easy banter by Amanda and Jewel, the two black girls on the team. Julie was relaxed and happy as she enjoyed her new friends.

"Hey, team!"

Everyone stopped talking as Carla raised her voice to get everyone's attention.

"The party is at Bill's house tonight. Is everyone going to be there?"

Julie waited to see everyone's response. Was this

a team thing? Did they all party on Friday nights? As she looked around the room she realized she was the only person who hadn't been on the team last year.

Most girls nodded. Amanda seemed to be the only one not going along with the plan.

"I won't be there tonight, gang," Amanda said. "My parents are going out of town for the weekend and I have to take care of my little brother and sister."

The rest of the team booed until Carla raised her hand for silence. It was obvious she was the leader of the team. "We'll let you off the hook this time, Amanda, but if your parents ever go out of town and take your brother and sister, let us know. We'll raid your house for the next party."

Then she turned and looked directly at Julie with a challenge in her eyes. "What about you, Julie? Will you be there? It's a team tradition to celebrate big on the final day of tryouts."

Julie swallowed the lump in her throat and tried to keep her voice steady. She wanted to fit in on the team. She didn't want to be the only oddball. "I didn't know about the tradition. I'm sorry, but I already have plans for the night."

Carla dropped her polite facade and sneered, "Going out with your boyfriend tonight?"

Julie was taken aback by her obvious hostility, but tried not to show it. "Well, yes."

"Are you going to some kind of church thing?"

Julie could feel her anger rising but struggled to

keep her voice casual. Why did Carla have to make such a big deal of it? "No, we're not." She didn't add that she didn't think it was any of her business. She could feel Jennifer watching her closely.

Carla seemed to be waiting for Julie to say more, and looked disappointed when she didn't. Shrugging, she turned to Sandy and laughed.

Julie turned away with her face burning and began to gather her things together. She saw Jennifer eye her with sympathy. Julie was confused. Jennifer seemed so nice. Why did she hang around with this crowd? She almost opened her mouth to invite her to the ski retreat with the youth group. Carla's next words stopped her.

Carla had turned back to Sandy, and now they both looked at Julie. Carla spoke in a voice loud enough for the whole locker room to hear. "She's a good tennis player, but that's about all she has going for her. That boyfriend of hers is the one who tried to kill himself with all those pills a couple months ago. Their Christianity doesn't seem to have done him much good!"

Julie gasped as the words dug straight into her already tender heart. Tears filled her eyes as she grabbed up her bag and headed for the door. She wanted to say something—anything—to defend what she had always believed and stood for, but there were no words. Blindly, she pushed through the door to close out the silence that had fallen on the room. All she could think of was escape.

FIVE

All Julie wanted to do was burrow under her covers and never come out when the alarm went off at 5 o'clock the next morning. A glance out her window showed a cold, cloudless sky glimmering with countless stars. Julie groaned. She hated getting up when it was dark. Why in the world was she doing this? Then she remembered. She was going skiing! That was enough to make her swing her legs out from under the covers and dash for the bathroom down the hall.

As she allowed the pulsating heat of the shower to slowly wake her fatigued body, her mind played over the night before. She wouldn't put it down as one of the best nights of her life. Carla's cutting words had seared their way into her heart and thoughts. They had repeated themselves over and over like a broken record. She and Kelly had planned a fun evening for the guys, but Julie just couldn't bring herself to be lots of fun. She had lied about having a headache and begged to just veg out in front of a video and make cookies. The other three had willingly agreed and had not seemed to notice her pensive mood. The guys that was. Julie had caught Kelly watching her several times during the night and knew she was wondering what was going on. They had cut the night short because they had to get up so early. Julie had escaped to her house with relief. Laying in bed last night she had thought about the party all of her teammates were at. What was it like? What were they doing? Was anyone getting drunk? What was Jennifer doing? The questions had rampaged in her mind.

It had taken her forever to get to sleep because she couldn't cut off the tape player in her head. She had almost decided to fake being really sick to get out of going to the retreat. She just didn't want to hear a lot of God stuff right now. But the lure of skiing was too much. The last time she had looked at her clock it had said 1 o'clock.

Julie climbed out of the shower and dried herself briskly with a fluffy towel. Her body wasn't really ready to be awake, but the shower had helped.

"Ready for some breakfast, Julie?"

"Mom!" Julie opened the door and peered out. "What in the world are you doing up? You didn't have to get up to fix me breakfast. I was just going to grab some cereal. The gang is picking me up at ten till seven."

"I know, honey. I hadn't planned on getting up but I woke up early so I thought I'd send you off with a good meal. I know you. If you eat a bowl of cereal you'll be starving in two hours. I've got some pancakes cooking downstairs."

Julie smiled her appreciation. "Thanks, Mom. That sounds great. I'll be right down."

It took her just a few minutes to slip into insulated underwear, ski bibs, and a wool sweater. She had packed her bag on Thursday night so all she had to do was throw in some toiletry items. Just before she zipped her bag she grabbed her Bible off the nightstand. She had thought about leaving it at home but after all, this was a youth retreat. She would have it, but she didn't have to read it. Lacing on hiking boots over thick wool socks, she grabbed her ski jacket out of the closet and clomped down the stairs.

"Are you trying to make sure the rest of the house gets to enjoy the early morning hours too, dear?"

"Sorry, Mom. I guess I could have taken the stairs a little quieter." Walking over to the kitchen counter, Julie gave her mom a quick hug and then loaded her plate with four steaming, fluffy blueberry pancakes. Looking at her watch she saw she had 15 minutes before Brent picked her up. It didn't take long to demolish the delicious stack. She hadn't eaten much of anything last night after Carla's cutting comments. Sleep had taken some of the edge off the words, but they still burned in her mind.

"Are you okay, Julie?"

Good grief! Were her feelings that obvious? Julie didn't want to talk about what she was feeling. She forced a tired smile to her face. "Just tired I guess, Mom. It's been a long week."

Her mother nodded. "Are you sure you should go on the retreat? I don't want you to get sick."

Julie gulped the rest of her milk and nodded. "I'll be fine, Mom. I'm young, remember? I can handle all these long hours."

Just then a knock sounded at the door. Julie pulled on her jacket, grabbed her bag, and gave her mom a quick kiss on the cheek. "See you tomorrow night, Mom. Thanks again for breakfast."

"You're welcome. Have a great time and be careful."

Julie was laughing as she got in the car.

"What's so funny?"

Julie turned to answer Kelly, who sleepily leaned against Greg's shoulder in the backseat. "What was the last thing Peggy said to you when you left today?"

Kelly thought for a moment. "I think she told me to be careful."

"What about you, Greg?" Julie asked.

"I think my mom said the same thing."

"Mine, too," Brent added.

Julie laughed again. "It's a parent thing, I guess. I wonder if they think we're going up there with some intention of trying to hurt ourselves. Besides that, we're young. We're not supposed to think about being careful. We're supposed to go have fun!"

Brent laughed along with her. "Be careful is the
last thing my mom always says to me. I think she
was especially nervous about my going skiing. She
still has pretty vivid memories of the last time we all
went skiing. Not that we plan on getting trapped by
a blizzard again!"

Julie nodded but thought about what he said. Her
mom had actually done pretty well. Mrs. Parker
had been really scared when the foursome had been
lost on the mountain in a blizzard just last month.
Julie was sure her mom wouldn't have been excited
about them going if it was just the four of them, but
they were going as a whole group. All of their time
would be spent downhill skiing anyway.

There were 40 kids milling around in the parking
lot of the church when they arrived. The Winter Ski
Retreat was always the largest. Kids who weren't
big on church would always show up to go skiing.
In the past Julie had always brought friends as a way
of sharing her faith in the Lord with them. Looking
around she noticed a lot of new faces. Jennifer's face
flashed in her mind, but she couldn't imagine having asked her to come. It was going to be tough
enough to fit in on the team without being religious.
Besides, she didn't have to play the "Christian
Game" on the team. They didn't care what she
thought about God. And since Julie didn't really
know anymore, that was just fine with her!

"Okay, everyone. I'm going to go down the list
of names. After I call your name you can go ahead

and get on the bus. We're actually on time. I bet God is as surprised as I am!"

The whole group laughed at Martin Stokes's comical expression. Julie loved her youth director and always had great fun with him. She had been coming to this church for six years and had learned a lot from him. She didn't think she wanted to hang around him much this weekend, though. He had this habit of asking how she was doing with the Lord. She for sure didn't want to have to answer that one!

Julie clambered on the bus close behind Kelly and found a seat for Brent and herself. Kelly and Greg were further in the back of the bus, but that was fine. The foursome loved to be together but they also had a lot of other friends in the youth group and didn't want people thinking the two couples were exclusive.

"I heard the weather report on the way over here. The snow is supposed to be awesome. Wintergreen is reporting their best February ever!"

Julie turned toward Pamela Parkinson, a shy sophomore at Kingsport High. "That's great, Pamela! I'd heard it was good but I didn't get the weather this morning. Have you skied much?"

Pamela shook her head. "Only a few times. The last time I went I finally got off the beginner slope and actually survived the intermediate slope. How about you?"

"About the same. I've gotten pretty good at cross-country skiing, but I've only been downhill skiing a few times as well. I can handle most of the intermediate slopes, but I'm sure my grace and style are sorely lacking," Julie laughed. "I just go to have fun. Brent assures me he's going to have me going down an expert slope today, but I'm not sure I'm ready for my parents to sign my death certificate!"

"What's this talk about dying?"

Pamela laughed up at Brent. "Julie said you were trying to kill her by getting her to go down one of the expert slopes."

"Not so!" Brent protested. "Julie never believes she can do something until you make her do it. She just needs a little more self-confidence. By the way, Pamela, did you know you're talking to a member of the Kingsport High Tennis team?"

Pamela turned to Julie with excitement. "You made it! Congratulations!"

"Thanks, Pamela." Julie returned the girl's smile but at the mention of the tennis team, Carla's words had come roaring back into her mind. She hoped she would be able to push them far enough back to have a good time this weekend.

• • •

Julie carried her skis and boots outside looking for a place to put everything on.

"Over here, Julie," Kelly called.

Julie looked over to see her friend sitting next to Greg on a bench. Walking over to join them, she deeply inhaled the fresh air. It was a perfect day.

The sky was a clear, deep Carolina blue. There was not one cloud to mar its perfection. The sun was shining brightly enough to raise the temperature to the 40 degrees predicted for the afternoon. There had been a big snow the weekend before and the snow blowers had been working ever since to deepen the base. The ski conditions were excellent.

Brent joined them and within minutes they were headed to join the line at the ski lift. Thankfully it wasn't very long and moved quickly. That was one thing Julie liked about Wintergreen. They would only let a certain number of people through the gates. That way it never got too crowded. Julie had been skiing once where there were so many people it just wasn't fun. She'd had to wait an hour in line and then skied down with what seemed like millions of people all around her.

Julie gazed down on the winter wonderland as the ski lift carried them high above the ground. The glare of the white, powdery snow was almost blinding as it reflected the brilliant sun. Tall evergreens cradled snow blown from the machines during the night. Flashes of color lent life to the scene as skiers flashed down the slopes. Julie could feel the excitement in her rising. She loved to ski, even if she wasn't all that good at it.

"Which slope?" Brent asked.

"Let's go down the Carolina. At least I've done that one before."

"Okay. We'll spend the morning on the interme-

diate slopes. But after lunch we're going to try one
of the expert. Game?"

Julie hesitated. Was she really ready to ski one of
the expert slopes?

Kelly had skied up from the lift just as Brent
posed his question. "You're ready for it, Julie. And
remember, you don't have to look good. You just
have to be able to get down it. I'm sure lots of people laughed at me my first try down Eagle's Nest,
but the feeling of having done it was worth it!"

Julie took courage from Kelly's encouragement.
She nodded slowly. "Okay. I'll try . . . but only if
you promise not to laugh!"

"That a girl!" Brent said. Pushing off on his skis
he yelled back over his shoulder, "Beat you to the
bottom!"

Julie, Kelly, and Greg were right behind him
when they got to the bottom.

"Wow!" Julie exclaimed. "I actually feel comfortable on these things. Usually it takes me a while to
get the hang of it again."

Greg nodded. "All the cross-country skiing you
did over Christmas helped a lot. It may be different,
but it built your confidence. That makes a huge difference."

The rest of the morning flew by as the four
friends attacked the slopes with gusto. After lunch,
Brent directed the three of them to the chair lift for
the advanced slope.

Julie gulped when she saw the sign for Eagle's

Nest. "You really think I can do Eagle's Nest without killing myself, huh?"

"No problem!" Brent returned cheerfully. "Looking down can be scary, but once you actually take off it's not that big of a deal. You ski the big ones just like you ski the other ones."

Minutes later Julie was taking deep breaths to control her fear. She felt like she was on top of the world staring down at a sheer drop off. She could feel her stomach tying into thousands of knots. Forcing a nervous laugh, she said, "You want to repeat the part about it not being a big deal once you take off?" Her voice ended on a high squeak.

She was grateful Brent didn't laugh at her. Taking her arm he turned her to face him and looked into her eyes. "I know it looks high, but I promise you it's not that bad. I wouldn't let you do something to hurt yourself. All you have to do is take it slow and easy. Just get down it. You'll build your confidence a little at a time. Soon you'll be blasting down it."

Julie's look of disbelief spoke more than any words. She couldn't imagine herself *ever* blasting down it. "Okay . . ." Looking over at Greg and Kelly she said, "Y'all go on down ahead of us. I don't want to slow you down and I'll be less nervous if I only have one person watching my descent. I'll meet you at the bottom." Looking down the slope again, she muttered, "Hopefully."

Greg and Kelly skied off and were soon little dots on the slope. Julie took a deep breath, smiled at

Brent, and pushed off. At first she kept her skis in a constant snow-plow position in order to slow herself. Gradually she realized Brent had been right. It looked terrifying, but she could do it. As she began to relax, her whole body loosened and she began to move in harmony with her skis. Halfway down she looked up and grinned at Brent.

"I'm doing it!" she yelled.

"I told you!" Brent called back. "Follow me!" Moving out in front of her he allowed his speed to increase a little.

Julie concentrated on doing just what he did. Her concentration was so intense that she was at the bottom before she even realized it. She laughed as her three friends cheered and clapped.

"Gosh, Julie. You looked like a pro up there," Greg said.

"Hardly!" Julie laughed. "But it was fun! Let's do it again."

Brent gave her a hug and then headed for the ski lift. "Let's go! We've only got two hours of skiing left. I don't want to miss any of it."

Julie was right behind him.

● ● ●

Julie fought to keep her eyes open as Martin rose to speak. The day had been wonderful but she was exhausted. The intense exercise, combined with her lack of sleep from the night before, had taken its toll. She could barely stay awake. She let her eyes roam around the room in an effort to not embarrass herself by falling asleep.

Blue Ridge Camp was a great place. The youth group had been here before. It was one of the few mountain camps that was open year round. Or at least a part of it was. The youth group was staying in the big main lodge. Made of logs, it was rustic both inside and out with a huge stone fireplace in the meeting room. There were dorm type rooms on each floor. The girls had the upstairs, the boys were downstairs. Also on the bottom level was a large, well-equipped kitchen with picnic tables scattered around the dining area. Julie's favorite part was the central area where everyone was now gathered. Huge beams caught the flickering firelight and cast it back down toward the floor. The floors were polished hardwood with thick rugs scattered around. The furniture was crafted from logs as well, and covered with large, soft, colorful cushions. The place was beautiful but virtually indestructible. A pool table and ping pong table were in one corner and a large table covered with games and puzzles occupied another. Groups who used the camp in the winter usually just needed lodging near the ski slopes. There were no activities offered. Julie loved it this time of the year because it was so quiet and peaceful.

"I know all of you must be really tired."

Julie nodded in agreement with Martin's first words. She didn't know if she could force herself to remain awake. His next words were welcome indeed.

"It's been a long day and we got back from the slopes more than an hour later than we had planned. I can tell by the bleary eyes looking up at me that even if I talked about what I had planned tonight, none of you would hear it. So I'm going to do my ego and you guys a big favor. I'm going to call off the meeting for tonight and let you go to bed."

He grinned as a chorus of thanks rose from the group gathered around him. "On one condition . . ."

Everyone grew quiet again.

"You have to really go to bed. I don't want there to be a sudden spurt of energy that will keep you up talking all night. If there is to be a spurt it can happen now. What's it going to be?"

"Bed!"

"Bed."

"All I want is my bed."

"Sleep!"

"Any dissenting voices?" Martin asked. Silence met his smiling glance. "Good! To bed we go. I'm as tired as the rest of you. Anything I have to say can be better said and heard tomorrow. Good night. Lights out in 30 minutes."

In less than ten minutes, Julie was fast asleep.

• • •

As soon as the afternoon meeting was over, Julie headed out the lodge door and down her favorite path. Martin had said they had an hour before they would load on the bus. She needed some time alone.

Striding determinedly down the trail she didn't look back to see if her friends were looking for her. If they were, she didn't want them to join her. The trail was only about a quarter of a mile long. Julie stepped out onto the ledge of rocks overlooking the valley. Allowing the wind to whip at her body, she stood braced to allow the gusts to tear at her thoughts as well.

The whole day had been a drain. She shouldn't have come. The skiing had been wonderful, but today had done nothing but show her over and over how confused she was. She was pretty sure she had played the game well, but she was exhausted. The singing and the skits had lost their appeal and whatever Martin had shared had been totally lost on her. She had plastered an attentive look on her face and had zoned out. Her thoughts had been occupied with the tennis team, ideas of partying, and the never ending mental tape of the words Carla spoke Friday afternoon.

The wind ripping at Julie's body seemed to tear at her heart as well. Carla had been right. Christianity hadn't done Brent much good. He had still tried to kill himself. And would have if Greg hadn't been there to save him by calling the paramedics. What good was faith in God if it wouldn't hold you up during the hard times? Maybe it didn't really make any difference. Everyone just lived their lives the best they could, whether they believed in God or not. And besides, couldn't you believe in

God and not have it dictate how you lived? Who really cared what you did? Shouldn't everyone be free to live however they wanted?

The questions raged through Julie's mind. Would she ever find answers? The majesty of the mountains had always calmed her before. They just added to her confusion now. How could she doubt there was a God when she had such creative evidence spread before her? This magnificent splendor could not just be a mistake or the result of a big explosion. But if there was a God, why couldn't he have helped Brent before he tried to kill himself? Why couldn't he have kept Kelly's mom from dying of cancer? What kind of God was he?

The buffeting of the wind began to win out against the thickness of her ski jacket. She didn't have enough layers to stand out here in the minus zero wind chill factor. Glancing at her watch, Julie realized she had stared out at the valley for over 30 minutes. She had just enough time to get back to the lodge, grab her stuff, and climb on the bus.

Her thoughts continued to race as she sped back to the lodge. She had had fun with Brent the day before, but she wasn't sure how she felt about their relationship. He was a constant reminder of all she was struggling with. And besides, dating him made life on the tennis team harder for her.

Julie's walk had accomplished nothing. All it did was increase her questions and confusion.

SIX

"Listen up, girls."

Julie and Jennifer stopped talking and turned toward Mrs. Crompton.

"First things first. I am no longer Mrs. Crompton. Now that we're all teammates, you can call me Coach. It's a lot easier and it doesn't make me feel so old."

Julie laughed and nodded with the rest of them. She was glad to be back at school and tennis practice. Plunging back into all the activity had silenced the questions. She was here to play tennis.

"We have three weeks until the first match. It may sound like a long time, but we have a lot of work to do. We're going to do drills until you want to scream. We're going to run until you think your feet are going to fall off. We're going to look for your particular area of weakness and do what's necessary to strengthen it. And we're going to determine what number you are on the team. Our first match is against Fulton High. They beat us last year, but just barely. I think we can take them this year. In fact, I'm predicting the best year this team has ever had."

Julie looked around in surprise when several of her teammates laughed softly.

Coach laughed with them. "Okay, okay. I know what you're thinking. You hear me say that every year. But it does get better every year. I have strong players that keep coming back, and I keep finding strong, new talent."

Julie blushed as Coach Crompton's eyes rested on her briefly. Her pleasure was short lived when she saw anger flash in Sandy's and Carla's eyes from where they sat watching her. Jennifer must be right. They must be jealous. For the first time Julie did nothing to conquer her feelings of anger. She stared back at the pair. She was here to play tennis. She would play to the best of her ability. Too bad if they didn't like it. She didn't want to be their enemy, but she also wasn't going to wilt before them. She hadn't done anything to deserve the treatment she was getting. She pulled her attention back to the coach.

"I am going to put six of you on three courts to play. Five of you will be with me on the other court to run through skills. We'll switch around for about an hour-and-a-half. Then we'll do drills and running for another 45 minutes. We'll finish up with a short meeting to answer any questions or hear any comments. We practice every day from 2:30 to 5 o'clock. I expect your best efforts during that time. If you can't make it there had better be a good reason. We have a lot of work to do." She paused and looked around. "Are there any questions now?" Silence. "No? Well, then let's get to it." She read who was to go where and began to walk toward court one.

Julie looked at Jennifer and laughed. "Looks like we have our work cut out for us."

Jennifer nodded. "She's tough, but she's good. She's only been here three years but boy, have we improved. The last school she was at in Kentucky won three state championships. That's what she wants for us."

Julie settled into the new schedule quickly. It was Wednesday before she knew it. Practice had gone well that afternoon, but she wanted to do some more work on her backhand. She approached Jennifer just as they were headed for the locker room.

"Have any energy left?"

"I might," Jennifer replied. "What do you have in mind?"

"I'd like to work on my backhand some more."

Jennifer looked at her incredulously. "You want to play more tennis? Are you nuts? Did Coach Crompton not run you to death enough?"

Julie shrugged and laughed. "Just call me motivated."

"I think crazy would be more fitting," Jennifer stated. "Besides, we can't play anymore right now.

The school just has it reserved until 5 o'clock. It's only open to members right now."

"I'm a member. I can play now if I want to. And," she added for enticement, "if you play with me you'll get to use the Jacuzzi you've been drooling over the last ten days."

Jennifer had been about to refuse, but the lure of the Jacuzzi was too much. "My body is going to hate me for this. I just hope the Jacuzzi will make up for it. Let's go crazy woman!"

An hour later Julie was satisfied with the progress she had made. Minutes later she and Jennifer sighed with ecstasy as they slid beneath the bubbling, steamy water of the Jacuzzi. Julie leaned back as she felt her muscles begin to loosen and let her entire body relax. She was playing good tennis and she knew it. She was going to enjoy her reward. For just a moment she thought about the Bible Study at church that would start in an hour. It had always been one of her favorite times of the week and normally she wouldn't miss it.

But things had changed. She slid further into the water and put it out of her mind. She knew her parents would wonder, but she was confident she could use the excuse of tennis and homework for a while.

• • •

"Happy Valentine's Day, Julie!"

"Thanks, Amanda. Same to you!" Julie responded as she placed her tray on the lunch table. She had gotten there earlier than her three tablemates.

"Happy Valentine's Day, Julie."

Julie smiled up at Jennifer who was headed over to sit with three more of the tennis team. Her new friend looked cute in denim jeans and a matching denim shirt. "Same to you, Jennifer. See you at practice this afternoon."

Julie sat down and broodingly waited for Brent and the others to join her. She caught herself watching her teammates wistfully. She was having great fun playing on the tennis team and wanted to get to know everyone better. Besides, she was feeling increasingly uncomfortable around her other friends. They had teased her Thursday about missing Bible Study. She had wanted to blurt out that she didn't ever want to come again but instead, she had smiled and explained about her schedule.

They wanted to talk about what was going on in youth group and Julie could care less. The intensity of her feelings surprised her, but she didn't know what to do about them. Her friends were still special to her and she didn't want to lose them, but she also wanted to be friends with the tennis team. Julie was afraid always being seen with "church kids" would make that harder.

Jewel, who had walked over to join Jennifer and her bunch, looked toward Julie and waved. Julie returned the greeting and then impulsively jumped up to join the girls. She left her tray on the table so Brent and the others would know she was returning, and walked over. She was pleased at the eager reception she received.

"Hi, Julie!" was the chorus that rose from the table.

"Hi, everyone." Julie slid into a seat and was soon deep in conversation about the tennis team. It was ten minutes before she remembered eating and returned to her table.

Brent seemed to be fine with her temporary desertion. "Hi, Julie. Think you can handle cold chicken? I thought about eating it for you, but didn't want to lose a hand."

Julie smiled, but shrugged. "I got it because it was the only thing that looked edible. Chicken just doesn't seem to cut it for me today."

"Are you ready for tonight?"

Julie was trying to be excited about the big Valentine's date. She really was looking forward to it. She didn't know what was the matter with her lately. Everything seemed to have lost its glow.

"I think so, Kelly. It's kind of hard to know if I'm ready when I have no idea what we're doing!"

Brent and Greg exchanged triumphant grins. They were obviously proud of their well kept secret.

Kelly turned to them. "Aren't you at least going to give us a clue?"

"Nope!" Greg responded. "Just show up dressed in the normal stuff and we'll take it from there."

Julie and Kelly exchanged quizzical glances. They were a little surprised they were supposed to show up in jeans and sweaters. They had thought the guys were going to tell them to dress up and take them out to a fancy restaurant. Obviously not.

• • •

Julie had left tennis practice and gone directly to Kelly's. She was relieved that no one had asked her to a party that night. She thought she was relieved anyway. Actually there had been a twinge of disappointment. She knew she wasn't going to go, but at least she wanted to be able to say no. Maybe everyone had already decided that she was too religious to join in their fun. She was surprised how much that bothered her.

"What sweater are you wearing tonight?"

"My blue one," Kelly responded. "I thought about wearing my red one because it's Valentine's Day, but Greg loves me in blue so I decided to wear that instead. How about you?"

"I decided to go red. But I think you made the right decision. Greg always seems to melt when he sees your eyes reflecting the blue in that sweater."

Kelly blushed, but smiled. "How is tennis going?"

"Great! I've been working pretty hard and it seems to be paying off. The coach made a special point today of telling me how glad she is I'm on the team."

"That's great, Julie! Hey, how are things going with Carla and Sandy? I haven't heard you say much about them lately."

Julie nodded. "I know. They seem to have laid

off. They don't say much of anything. Coach had
me play Carla the other day and I actually beat her.
I thought she was going to be furious, but she just
seemed really surprised. I think my being a good
tennis player is helping a little."

"That's good. I've been praying for you about
that."

"Thanks." Julie didn't know what else to say.

"Have you had a chance to ask Jennifer to come
to church yet?"

Julie wanted to scream. This was Valentine's
Day. She didn't want to talk about church stuff. She
stuffed down her feelings and managed a smile.
"Not yet. I'm waiting for just the right time. I know
God will open the door for me." She wanted to
laugh at her own hypocrisy. Then she decided it
wasn't funny.

They were ready when the boys arrived at 7
o'clock. Both looked sharp in their jeans and red
sweaters. Kelly called good-bye to her family and
they disappeared out the door.

Both girls were surprised when Greg pulled
his car up in front of the indoor putt-putt place. They
looked at each other silently. This was their fabulous
Valentine's Date? They loved putt-putt, but . . .
Without words they agreed to make the best of it.

And Julie had to admit it was fun once she got
over the disappointment. They played two rounds.
She and Brent won the first one, Greg and Kelly the
second.

"Okay, time to go."

Julie looked at Brent in surpise. "We're tied. What do you mean it's time to go? Aren't we going to do the best of two out of three?"

"Nope. Not enough time. Our ride is waiting."

Now Julie and Kelly really *were* confused. Julie spoke for them both. "What do you mean our ride is waiting?"

"Exactly what he said," Greg said and grinned widely. "Get your coats, ladies. It's time to go."

"Do I have time to go to the restroom?" Julie asked with a smile. She didn't know what the boys were up to but she was willing to play the game their way.

"Of course," Brent said. "I know better than to deprive a female of bathroom privileges. I learned that from my mother."

Julie and Kelly both laughed, stuck out their tongues, and walked haughtily away.

They were talking about the boys' secret when the door to the bathroom opened and Sandy and Carla walked in with a couple of their friends.

"Hi, Julie."

Julie looked up in surprise. "Hi, Carla. Hi, Sandy. What are you guys doing here?" Putt-putt didn't seem to be their style.

Carla spoke up. "We stopped to get a pizza. This place may be a dive but they make great pizza."

Julie ignored the subtle dig.

Carla continued. "And besides. We need to doctor our soft drink cans." Laughing, she popped the lid off of her soda can and poured the drink down the drain. Sandy and their friends followed suit. Reaching into her bag she pulled out four bottles of beer and passed them around.

Julie and Kelly watched quietly while they washed their hands.

Opening the bottles, Carla and her friends carefully poured the beer into the empty soda cans and then buried the bottles under paper in the trash can. Laughing they raised their cans against each others and headed for the door. Carla stopped and looked back.

"You're welcome to join us, Julie. We're headed over to a great party after we eat our pizza. How about it?"

Julie was surprised at how much she wanted to say yes. She was very aware of Kelly by her side. Shaking her head she said, "No thanks, Carla. I have plans for tonight."

Carla just laughed, waved her hand, and disappeared through the swinging door.

Silence fell on the white, tiled bathroom.

"Well!" Kelly said. "Can you imagine spending an evening with them?"

Julie shook her head in amusement, but secretly she was getting to the point where she very definitely could imagine it. She wanted to know what they did. She wanted to be a part of their world and see what it was like.

"Let's go, Kelly. The guys are waiting!" She

feigned excitement and pulled her friend from the bathroom. She tried to ignore her teammates in the corner.

"Okay, turn around and close your eyes."

"What?" Julie asked Brent. "What are you talking about?"

He took her shoulders and turned her around before she reached the door to the parking lot. Greg grabbed Kelly and did the same. Then they reached in their pockets and pulled out bandanas.

"You'll need to wear these for a while, ladies."

Kelly stared at Greg as he spoke, but laughed. "For how long a while, sir?"

"Oh, until we tell you you can take them off."

Both girls shook their heads, but they were enjoying the mystery. It was almost enough to take Julie's mind off the scene back in the pizza parlor. The girls succumbed and were led out into the cold night air.

Moments later they were told to step up, felt warm air rush against their faces, heard a large door clanging shut, and were cut off from the night sounds. They were led over to something large and soft, told to sit, and then silence fell. Several minutes passed and then they heard an engine throb to life. Whatever they were in now began to move. During this time, the boys had said nothing.

Julie sat quietly, trying to figure out what they were in. It was obvious it was some kind of large vehicle, but she had no idea what it meant. They rode quietly for about 20 minutes. The only sound was an occasional snicker from either Greg or Brent. The vehicle they were in turned off the road and then seemed to bump over some kind of field. Julie's curiosity was growing. Where were they? She didn't have to wait long for her answer.

Minutes later the vehicle stopped moving. She heard a sound like a striking match and then felt the blindfold being removed from her eyes.

Julie and Kelly gasped with astonishment. They were in the back of some kind of big truck, but it was none they had ever seen. Two sofas lined either side, piled high with cushions and blankets. In the middle was a low standing table covered with a white tablecloth and decorated with four flickering red and white candles and a bouquet of pink carnations. There were pictures hanging on the wall and a thick bear-skin rug lying in front of the door.

The two girls looked at each other speechless. Just when Julie felt questions forming on her tongue, more surprises hit her. With a mighty heave from outside the back door swung open.

"Mom! Dad!" Julie squeaked.

"Dad! Peggy!" Kelly managed behind her. "What in the world are y'all doing here?"

"Where is here?"

The Parkers laughed at their daughter's words. "Here is the newly reopened Kingsport Drive-In. We are your servants for the evening. Dinner will be served soon." Then they turned with the

Marshalls and disappeared.

Julie turned to Brent in a daze.

His grin widened at her expression. "Surprised?"

"Overwhelmed would be more adequate. How in the world did you and Greg do this? And what in the world are we in?"

Kelly nodded. "Those questions would do for starters!"

Brent laughed. "I'll answer the second question first. We are in a moving van. We talked to your Dad and he worked it out. I had heard him say something about having a friend who owned a moving company, so . . ."

Greg jumped in at that point. "And we did it with a lot of help. Julie's Dad set up the truck. Our folks let us steal furniture to put in here."

Kelly interrupted. "I thought I recognized the bearskin rug from in front of your fireplace."

Greg nodded. "It all came from a few different places. Julie, your Dad is driving this thing. Kelly, your Dad is keeping him company. And your moms have prepared dinner and are going to serve it. My parents were bummed that they were going to be left out but they had to go out of town."

Brent nodded. "Mine, too. We're going to all have to endure pictures so that my mom can see what we did with the truck."

Kelly laughed. "Where in the world did you come up with such a great idea?"

Greg grinned sheepishly. "Well, I was listening

the other night when you said you were going to
have to go to the library and find a date book to
come up with ideas. I thought that idea itself was a
great one, so I went and did some research. The
original idea was to rent a U-Haul truck. That was
definitely out of our budget, but with a little cre-
ativity we pulled it off. Not bad, huh?"

The girls laughed with delight.

Julie was the first to speak. "This is awesome,
guys. I can't believe you went to all this trouble for
us." For the moment she had forgotten her irrita-
tion with Brent and her desire to be with her other
friends.

Kelly smiled softly at Greg. "You were right.
This is the most perfect Valentine's date ever.
Thank you."

Just then Peggy and Mrs. Parker rounded the corner.

Peggy spoke in a properly formal voice. "Dinner
is served."

The boys sprang to attention and seated the girls
on the sofas in front of their dinner places. Leaning
over, Greg hit the button to the concealed tape player and soft music filled the truck.

In just minutes they had spread before them an
elegant dinner of Shrimp Alfredo, a crisp green
salad, and fresh bread. When the meal had been
served, Kelly's father approached the table with
a bottle of sparkling apple cider and filled their
glasses.

Bowing low, he backed away from the table and out of the truck. "If you have need of anything, just let us know." Smiling, he disappeared along with the two women.

"This is too much!" Kelly muttered.

Julie nodded her agreement, smiled at Brent, and dug into the delicious meal.

Almost as if on cue, the movie started just as they were finishing their meal. Greg leaned forward and tapped lightly on the front of the truck. Moments later, Julie's father slipped in, cleared the table, told them to have a good time and vanished. The only evidence of his presence was the slam of the truck door as he climbed back in.

Mr. Parker had angled the truck just right to get the best view of the movie as it filled the big screen. Julie settled back against the sofa to enjoy *Sleepless in Seattle*. She had missed it the first time around and was glad to get to see it. Brent settled down next to her and then pulled blankets around them in order to keep warm. The truck had maintained its warmth through dinner, but the open bay door was causing it to chill rapidly. Julie snuggled into the warmth of the blankets gratefully.

The two hours passed quickly. Just as the final credits were rolling, Peggy appeared at the back of the truck with large slices of cheesecake topped with fresh strawberries. It didn't take long for the foursome to polish off the delicious dessert.

"This tastes like your mother's cheesecake, Brent."

"It is, Julie. This was the only thing she could contribute so she took extra time on it. I think it's the best she's ever made."

"So many people worked to make this possible," Kelly mused.

Greg nodded. "We couldn't have pulled it off without a lot of help. Your folks have been great. So have yours, Julie."

"Picture time!"

The four friends laughed as the four parents appeared at the back of the truck. They smiled and struck dramatic poses as the flash filled the truck with brilliant light again and again.

"I think we should get a picture of the parents in the back of this thing. After all, they made it possible."

Kelly quickly agreed. "What a great idea, Greg. Come on Peggy. Dad."

Julie chimed in to get her parents into the truck.

The four of them climbed out to make room for their parents. Kelly grabbed the camera.

Julie was the only one who saw the maroon van drive by. She didn't know the driver, but she recognized Carla, Sandy, Jennifer, and Jewel. She saw the beer bottles in their hands and heard their loud laughter. They seemed to be having a great time. Julie stared after the truck with a strange and sudden longing. She had had a great time tonight. But she wanted to see what their kind of fun was like.

She suddenly knew she wouldn't turn down another invitation.

SEVEN

J ulie was nervous as she pulled off her school clothes and slid into her tennis dress. Today was a big day. Coach Crompton was going to assign positions on the team at the end of practice. The first two weeks of practice had flown by. Julie had worked hard and knew she was playing the best tennis of her life. Jennifer had agreed to the additional hour of practice every day as long as she got to soak in the Jacuzzi for as long as she wanted. Julie was thrilled with the arrangement. She hadn't said anything to Coach Crompton about her extra hours, but she was pretty sure her coach knew.

"Big day, Julie!"

Julie lifted her head from tying her shoes and smiled at Jennifer. "You're right about that!"

Jennifer, already dressed and ready to go, sat down next to her. "Do you remember my prediction two weeks ago?"

Julie looked uncomfortable but nodded.

"Well, I meant it. I predict you will be one of the

top three seed on the team." Then she added smugly, "I'm very seldom wrong, you know."

Julie laughed. "Time will tell, Jenn. I'm just trying to focus on doing my best. I get too uptight when I think about what the results could be."

"Okay. You focus and I'll think about the results. That way I get to say I told you so!"

Julie laughed at her friend again and headed for the door to the courts. "Let's go warm up." Opening the door, she waited for Jennifer to follow.

They were the first ones there so they had the courts to themselves for ten minutes. Julie was glad for a chance to loosen up before playing. As she volleyed the ball across the net, she thought about her week. She knew tennis was consuming her life, but she wanted it that way. Wednesday night had found her just getting home before Bible Study started. She could tell her mother was concerned, but she hadn't said too much. Julie had explained she was extremely tired from tennis and had a lot of homework to do. Her mother had opened her mouth to say more, but changed her mind and turned away to finish dinner. Julie was grateful that she wasn't pushing her.

"Hello, Julie. Hi, Jennifer."

Julie looked up in surprise. Carla and Sandy had taken the court next to them. Carla was actually speaking nicely to her. "Hi, Carla. Hi, Sandy. How's it going?"

"Okay," Carla shrugged. "I saw Coach Crompton's list. You're playing Jewel first today, and then you're going to play the loser of Sandy's and my match."

Julie nodded. She didn't know what to say. It was hard to tell if Carla was angry about the possibility of having to play against her, or if she was just carrying on conversation. Coach Crompton cut off further thought.

"Let's go girls. Find your name on the list and take a court. Everyone plays for 30 minutes. Then you switch partners and go at it again. I know you're all probably nervous because I'll be choosing team positions today. Just remember to play the best you can, and let the results take care of themselves."

Minutes later Julie found herself faced off across the net from Jewel. The two smiled and then began to play. When the whistle sounded after 30 minutes, Julie was winning four games to one.

"You can beat Carla, Julie. Just concentrate!" Jewel encouraged her when she walked to the net to shake hands.

Julie nodded dubiously. "I'm not so sure I can beat her, but I'm going to give it my best shot. Thanks for the vote of confidence."

Jewel nodded. "Carla and Sandy have been at the top of the heap for too long. One of them needs to be brought down a little. I'm putting my vote on you to do it."

Julie just smiled and moved over to the next

court where Carla was waiting for her. She smiled at her opponent, but Carla just looked at her. Julie was surprised to see a nervous glint in the other girl's eyes. Settling down to receive Carla's first serve, Julie cleared her mind and resolved to play the best tennis she could.

Carla's first serve blistered into the far corner. Julie was ready for it and returned it low and fast over the net to her backhand. The battle was on. Sweat poured from both the girls as they struggled to gain dominance over the other. Julie won the first game. Carla took the next in a triple-deuce game. Julie handily won the third game.

Julie prepared to serve and watched her opponent carefully. Carla seemed to be flustered, and she was getting tired. Julie knew they would only have time for one more game. If she could win this one, she would take the number two position from Carla. Julie felt herself tighten with determination. She wasn't sure whether her resolve came from sheer competitiveness or the desire to best Carla because she had given her such a hard time. Whatever it was, she intended to win.

Pulling her arm back she leaned into her serve with all her strength. All the extra practice had paid off. The tennis ball met her racquet and flashed across the net. Carla wasn't able to reach it. Julie aced her! Carla's flustered condition increased. She returned Julie's next serve, but she didn't get back into position and Julie was able to blast it into a corner where she couldn't reach it. The rest of the game went quickly. Carla seemed to have lost heart.

The mini-set ended with Julie beating her three to one.

Julie couldn't help the glow of satisfaction that flowed through her. She knew she had a wide smile on her face as she walked forward to shake hands with Carla. It felt good to have won the second spot on the team.

Carla looked tired and disappointed, but she managed a smile. "Good playing, Julie."

"Thanks, Carla," Julie replied.

Carla turned to walk away, hesitated, and turned back. "I'm glad you're on the team, Julie."

Julie didn't know what to say. She was too surprised to talk.

Carla continued. "Sandy is having a party at her house tonight. Would you like to come?"

Julie could tell Carla expected her to say no. "Thanks, Carla. That sounds like fun. What time?"

Carla's eyes widened slightly, but she spoke casually. "Seven-thirty. The whole gang will be there."

Julie struggled to keep her voice light. "Okay. I'll be there. See you later."

"Yeah. See you later."

Julie watched Carla walk off. She had surprised even herself when she had said yes. But she had decided last week that she wouldn't turn down another invitation. She pushed aside the thought of the double date she was supposed to have with

Brent, Kelly, and Greg. She would call and cancel. They would just have to understand she needed to do something with the team. If they didn't understand, well . . . too bad. She had made her decision.

"You did it! I knew you could do it!" Just then Jennifer ran up to give her a big hug. Jewel was right behind her.

Julie grinned and laughed. "I suppose you're waiting to say I told you so."

Jennifer smiled back. "Well . . . I did tell you so! One day you'll learn to listen to me."

"Good playing, Julie." Just then Coach Crompton walked up to give her a handshake.

"Thanks, Coach."

"I guess you know this makes you number two on the team?"

Julie just nodded and grinned.

Coach Crompton laughed and turned away. "You earned it. Good job!"

Julie's glow lasted all the way into the locker room. She was getting ready for her shower when Carla called out the last announcement about the party.

"Don't forget everyone. Tonight. Sandy's house. The action starts at 7:30." She paused and then continued. "And our new number two player on the team will be there!"

Julie turned red but smiled as cheers rang through the locker room.

"You'll be there tonight?" Jennifer asked.

Julie nodded. She was surprised at the faint look of disappointment on Jennifer's face. It disappeared almost as fast as it had appeared. Maybe she had imagined it.

• • •

Julie breathed a sigh of relief as she crawled in the car with Jennifer. She hadn't known what to wear, but Jennifer's jeans and sweater convinced her she wouldn't be different from everyone else. As they headed to Sandy's she thought back to the conversation she had had with Brent an hour earlier. He had been disappointed when she broke their date but had been cool about it. She had just said that she really wanted to spend some time with her teammates. She had even added that the only way she would be able to share Christ with them was if she got to know them better. The lies were coming easier. She had felt uncomfortable but had managed to shake it off. She had set her course and nothing was going to change her mind.

Jennifer had come in to meet her parents and everything had gone smoothly. Julie had just said she and some of her team friends were going to hang out tonight. She had never lied to her parents about any of her activities before. She knew they trusted her. She hated doing it, but she didn't see any other way. Julie was glad when they drove up to Sandy's house. She wanted to leave her thoughts outside.

"Hi, Mr. Jones. Hi, Mrs. Jones!" Jennifer waved

brightly as she moved toward the stairs leading to the basement.

Julie was surprised to see Sandy's parents there. She thought kids only had parties when parents weren't home.

Jennifer noticed the surprise on Julie's face. "Sandy's parents are cool," she said as they moved down the stairs. "They let Sandy have parties here any time she wants to. They figure kids are going to drink so they might as well drink at home. They even help us buy the beer. They figure we'll be responsible enough not to drink and drive." Jennifer giggled. "Most of the time they're right. What they don't know won't hurt them."

Julie said nothing. She was just going to listen and learn. But she did intend to watch how much alcohol Jennifer drank before she got in the car with her to drive home.

"Hi, Julie!"

Julie waved to some of her teammates who were already there. The room was crowded with people she didn't know, as well. A lot of them she recognized from school. Some seemed to be college-aged. Loud music pulsated through the large, dimly lit room. The walls were lined with sofas and chairs that had been pushed out of the center of the room for the night. The floor was large enough for dancing, but there were only a few couples moving in time to the music. Most of the crowd seemed to be in one corner. It didn't take long to figure out why.

As the crowd separated for a moment, Julie caught a glimpse of a long table. It was easy to tell it was covered with six-packs of beer and wine coolers. Behind the table was a large refrigerator.

"Come on. Let's go get something to drink."

Julie allowed Jennifer to pull her across the room, but she had no intention of drinking. She just wanted to see what this was all about.

"Hi, good looking. Want a beer?"

Julie looked into the face of a senior she recognized from school. He was holding a beer but didn't seem to be drunk. It was probably too early in the night for that.

"No thanks," she said casually. Glancing around the table she saw that there were a few Cokes. "I'll just have a Coke."

The guy shrugged. "Okay. Hey, my name is Joe. I've seen you around school. Who are you?"

"My name is Julie."

"Well, hi, Julie. It's good to have you here. How did you get hooked up with this crowd?"

"I play on the tennis team with some of them at school."

Joe nodded eagerly. "You must be the new girl on the team. I've heard that some whiz has come along and stolen the number two position from Carla."

Julie didn't know what to say. Joe didn't seem to notice. He took another slug of his beer and turned to talk to one of his buddies. Julie took the opportunity to study the room. As far as she could tell she was the only one not drinking beer or wine, but nobody seemed to care.

"Hi, Julie. I'm glad you could make it."

Julie turned to speak to Carla. "Thanks, Carla." Then she stopped. She had never been good at small talk, and she definitely felt out of her element. Carla was the most relaxed she had ever seen her.

"I've been telling everyone how you stole the number two position from me. I've got some friends who are looking forward to meeting you. But be forewarned," she added in a friendly voice, "I'll try to take my position back."

Julie laughed. "No problem. I enjoy competition."

"Then this is the girl I wanted to meet."

Julie looked over Carla's shoulder at the tall, blond guy who had spoken. He was eyeing her with obvious interest. She expected the can of beer she saw in his hand.

Carla smiled and moved over to make room for him. "Julie, this is Marshall. He's a freshman at North Carolina State. He plays tennis for them, as well. He wanted to meet the girl who stole my position."

Julie smiled as Marshall shook her hand with courtly exaggeration. She was having a good time. What was the big deal about parties? Sure, people were drinking, but no one was drunk. Everyone was just standing around talking, or dancing. She felt herself relaxing and laughed naturally into

Marshall's blue eyes. She pushed thoughts of Brent out of her mind.

She talked easily with Marshall about tennis as she finished off her Coke. He noticed her empty can and took it from her to throw away.

"I'll be right back." Turning, he disappeared into the crowd. Moments later he appeared with a cold can of beer and handed it to her.

Julie opened her mouth to say no and then closed it. Reaching out, she took the beer. She didn't want to keep looking different from everyone else. She was having a good time. This was no big deal. She wasn't going to get drunk so what difference did it make. Tilting her head back she smiled at Marshall and then took a sip. She had never had beer before. She struggled to keep her face from showing how bad she thought it was. Why in the world did people drink this stuff? Tipping her can, she took another sip.

Within 20 minutes Julie had decided beer was something she could get used to. It was just a drink after all. And she liked the way it made her feel. Her insides were warm and comfortable and she found it easy to talk to the people who were coming up to meet her. She was definitely having fun.

● ● ●

Three hours later Julie was feeling more and more uncomfortable. Things had gotten out of hand. She had stopped at two beers and had gone

back to drinking Coke. As far as she could tell, she
was the only one who had done so. Except for
Jennifer. At one point in the night, Jennifer had
worked her way over to where Julie was talking to
Marshall and had pulled her aside.

"I've got to leave around 11. My parents are going
out of town in the morning and I have to take care
of my little brother and sister." With those words
she screwed up her face. "Definitely takes some of
the fun out of partying. I can't afford to have a hang-
over tomorrow. I usually get to sleep in so no one
knows what condition I come home in on Friday
night. Not this week, though. I don't want to have
to deal with my parents. Three is my limit for the
night."

Julie wanted to ask who drove her car when she
didn't have a limit, but she didn't. She was just
thankful she wouldn't have to worry about it
tonight.

Julie was ready to go home. Most of the lights
had been turned out, but she could watch the shad-
owed movement of couples in the corners. The
music was still loud but not loud enough to cover
the slurred yelling across the room as people tried to
talk. Conversation had grown crazier and crazier as
alcohol loosened tongues. She heard guys talking
about their exploits with their dates the week before
and listened to the girls rating the guys in explicit
language. Marshall had been really nice until he had
started to get drunk. At one point while they were

talking, he had grabbed her arm and leaned over to kiss her. The smell of his hot beer breath had almost gagged her. She had managed to dodge his kiss, laugh playfully, and divert his attention by turning to talk to someone else.

Now she was standing next to the table just watching. A glance at her watch told her it was almost 11. As if beckoned by her thoughts, Jennifer appeared next to her.

"You ready to go?"

Julie nodded in relief then looked at her friend closely. Her hair and clothes were disheveled and her voice seemed a little shaky. "Are you okay?"

"Oh sure," Jennifer laughed. "Marshall said you had given him the cold shoulder so I just made him feel a little better." The sadness in her brown eyes belied the lightness in her voice. "Anyway, it's time to go."

Julie climbed the stairs with mixed feelings. She had had fun until an hour or so ago. Maybe if she had drunk more beer she wouldn't have been uncomfortable. She tried to push away her impressions of how empty the whole crowd had seemed. It was a different world . . . meant to be lived by different rules.

EIGHT

Kelly laid her lunch tray on the table and looked around the dining hall for Julie. Several members of the tennis team were huddled in the corner laughing and talking, but she didn't see her friend. Just then Brent walked up with Greg.

"Hey, Brent. Where's Julie?"

Brent shrugged. "I don't know. She said something about needing to talk to her tennis coach when I saw her in English this morning. She must be running a little late."

Just then Kelly caught sight of Julie entering the line. Julie returned her wave and then took her place at the end. Kelly turned back to the two guys.

"I'm concerned about Julie. She just doesn't seem like herself anymore. She was at youth group last night, but she seemed to be in a different world."

Greg nodded. "Something is going on, that's for sure. Brent, do you know anything about that party she went to on Friday night?"

Brent looked uncomfortable. "Yeah. I heard some guys talking in the locker room in gym last period. Evidently it was quite a bash. They made it sound like everyone was plastered."

"Not Julie!" Kelly protested. "She wouldn't do that." But she was beginning to wonder. Julie had become more and more distant. Kelly hadn't really been surprised when she had cancelled their double date that Friday night. The three of them had gone skating without her, but she knew Brent had been hurt. What was going on with her friend? She'd never seen her act this way. She watched Julie weave her way through the crowd with her loaded tray. She also caught her eyeing her tennis teammates wistfully before she sat her tray on the table and gave them a bright smile.

Kelly knew the smile was fake. It reached her lips but it didn't extend to her eyes. "Hi, Julie."

"Hi, gang!" Julie said blithely. "This place is a zoo today. Must be the spring weather."

Winter weather would visit them again before the season was over, but North Carolina was enjoying a taste of spring for a couple of days. A warm front had blown up from the south the day before causing the temperature to soar to a balmy 70 degrees. Buds seemed to be straining against their confines, yearning to break forth into leaves and blossoms. Julie hoped they would stay wrapped in their protective covering a little while longer. Spring was her favorite time of the year. If the buds were too impatient, their fragile beauty would be destroyed by the cold weather that was sure to descend again. Soon it would be safe for them to burst out.

Kelly could tell Greg and Brent were uncomfortable and didn't know what to say. Their minds were focused on Friday night's party. Kelly's was too, but she wanted to be careful.

"We missed you Friday night, Julie." Kelly hadn't had much of a chance to talk to Julie at youth group the night before. Julie had gotten there late and had left early, giving some excuse about a test today.

Julie smiled. "Yeah. I missed being with you guys," she lied. "It was great to spend time with my teammates though. I feel like I'm getting to know them better." She was ready for their questions about Friday night. She had thought through her answers and was confident she could satisfy them.

Kelly continued. "How was the party?"

"Oh, the party was fine. Just a lot of talking and dancing. I met some great people." The image of Marshall's face as he had approached her with his hot beer breath flashed in her mind.

Kelly took a deep breath. "What was it like? Was there a lot of drinking and stuff?"

Ah, the question. Julie wasn't sure if Kelly would ask, but here it was. "Yeah," she shrugged. "I guess there was. But there was no pressure to take part. I just talked and stuff. One thing I realize is that if I'm going to have a chance to share about Christ with these people, I have to become their friend. But that doesn't mean I have to do what they do. It wasn't that bad. Just people trying to have a good time." She didn't volunteer her feelings of revulsion for the drunken behavior she had witnessed, or how dispirited and listless Jennifer had been on the way home. She also didn't talk about how long she had laid awake that night wondering what she was getting involved in. She was fitting in with the girls on the team. That's what she wanted. Wasn't it?

Kelly exchanged looks with Brent and Greg as Julie dug into her lunch. They all knew she was lying. Kelly could feel her concern growing, but she didn't know what to do.

Brent cleared his throat. "Greg and I have some great plans for Friday night." He forced his voice to be cheerful. "Want to hear them?"

Julie looked up absently. "I'm sorry, Brent, but I have other plans for Friday night. Friday is our first match. The team always has a big celebration afterward. I've promised them I'll come along." She hesitated at the hurt that flashed across Brent's face. "Why don't you come along? I think there is going to be a party at Carla's house. Her parents are going to be out of town."

Brent shook his head. "I don't think so, Julie. That's not really my scene. Maybe we can do something Saturday night."

"Maybe," Julie responded tightly. Why did Brent

have to be so rigid? It was just a party. Julie was surprised she had never noticed before how childish
Brent was sometimes. Pictures of Marshall flashed
through her mind again. But this time she just remembered the impression when she first met him. His big
blue eyes, his interest in her tennis playing, his warm
laugh. Honestly, Brent was just too religious for his
own good. Why couldn't he loosen up some?

Julie finished her lunch, chatted for a few minutes about an upcoming history test, and then left to
join her tennis team. Her friends watched her go in
silence.

• • •

Julie glanced up in the stands as she waited nervously for her first match. She couldn't believe that
three weeks of practice had flown by so quickly.
This was the real thing. She knew the number two
player for Fulton High was good. She had beaten
Carla the year before. Julie tried to force nervous
thoughts out of her mind. She waved at her parents
when they caught her eye and waved in her direction. Sitting below them a couple of levels were
Brent, Kelly, and Greg. Julie was grateful they had
come. They were good friends. At that thought she
began to feel uncomfortable about how she had
been treating them lately. She shook herself mentally. She couldn't start thinking like that. She had
to stay focused for the match.

She tried to remember everything Carla had told

her. Her opponent's name was Sarah. She was a senior and had played all four years in high school. Her backhand was her one weakness, even though Carla had laughingly said you could hardly call it a weakness. She had said though, that if Julie could play to it constantly it would start to wear her out. The trick was playing to it constantly. Sarah had an ability to keep you running so that she was in control of the play.

"How you feeling?"

Julie gave Jennifer a nervous smile. "About the way I look, probably."

Jennifer laughed. "Actually you look pretty cool over here. But you're human. You have to be pretty nervous about your first match on the team. And Sarah is good."

Julie gave a nervous groan. "I know. I know!" She shook her head. "All I can do is get out there and give it my best."

She felt a hand come down on her shoulder. Coach Crompton's voice sounded over her head. "That's all any of us can do, Julie. Just pretend this is practice. I want you to play well, of course. But mostly I want you to go out there and have fun. If you do that you'll relax and play tennis the way I know you can."

Julie took a deep breath and nodded. Just then her match was called. Tossing down her hand towel, she grabbed her racquet and walked over to the net to shake hands with her opponent. Sarah was medium height, with short brown hair and serious blue eyes. She gave Julie a smile and then turned to head toward her position.

Sarah had won the toss so she would serve first.

Julie balanced lightly as she waited for the serve. It came flying at her, she returned it to Sarah's backhand, and the match was on. They would play eight games. The winner would be determined by who took the most games.

An hour later, Julie felt like she had been run through a wringer. She had never played such hard tennis in her life. Her right arm, and her legs, were beginning to ache from exhaustion. Her one consolation was that Sarah looked as tired as she did. Each game had been long and drawn out. The points had been long battles and each game had locked at deuce several times before one finally bested the other. Julie couldn't believe it, but she was actually ahead four to three. If she could hang on for one more game she would win her match!

"Come on, Julie! You can do it!"

Julie flashed a tired smile toward the stands where Kelly, Brent, and Greg were cheering her on. Yells of encouragement were also coming from her teammates. All the other matches were already over. None had been such a battle as this one.

Julie was unaware that the entire match score was tied five to five. Whoever won this match would determine the outcome for her team. It was a good thing she didn't know, she told everyone later. If she had, she probably would have gotten nervous and blown the whole thing. Oblivious to the importance of the outcome, she just settled down to play her best tennis. She would pull up reserves of strength from somewhere.

It was her turn to serve. She put all of her flagging strength into it. Twenty minutes later it was all over. The game, as usual, had run to deuce several times. Julie had held on. Desperate to end the battle, knowing she would be out of strength soon, she gave the last serve her all. She watched as it skimmed low across the net and smashed into the near corner to Sarah's backhand. Sarah had reached the end of her energy. She made an effort to reach the ball, but her racquet barely tipped it. The ball dribbled to the net and lay there in defeat.

Julie stood stunned. She had actually done it! She had beaten the number two player from Fulton High. Seconds later she found herself surrounded by excited teammates!

"Way to go, Julie!"

"I knew you could do it!"

"You won the match for us!"

Julie looked questioningly at Jewel when she delivered the last comment. "Huh?"

"It's true!" Jewel said. "The match score was five to five. Your victory sent us over the tie. We've beaten Fulton for the first time in eight years!"

Julie grinned and reached gratefully for the water bottle Coach Crompton handed her. "Thanks."

"You played some fine tennis, Julie. I've never seen you play that well."

Julie knew she was right. The battle with Sarah had brought out abilities she didn't know she possessed. But the best thing was that she had had fun. Walking over to the other bench, she shook hands with her opponent.

Sarah looked up at her with a small smile. "I hate to be beaten, but you played some great tennis."

"Thanks, Sarah. I've never had to play so hard in my life. There's no telling what the outcome of our next meeting will be."

Sarah laughed. "Just be assured I'll be out for revenge!"

As Julie left the court she was surrounded by the rest of the foursome.

"Congratulations, Julie!" said Brent as he gave her a hug.

Kelly and Greg echoed his sentiments. It was obvious they were proud of her.

Julie felt a lump form in her throat at the loyalty of her friends. She was opening her mouth to say she had decided to go out with them that night instead of going to the party. She knew whatever they did, they would have fun. She never had the chance.

Carla appeared at her side. "Way to go, Julie. I don't think I could have beaten her. You did a great job!"

Julie smiled at her sincere words. "Thanks, Carla!"

Carla continued. "I'm really glad you're coming to the party tonight. It wouldn't be the same without you. You're a real part of the team now! See you later!"

Julie swallowed the words she was getting ready to say. "Yeah. See you later."

She turned to her friends and smiled awkwardly. "Well, I guess I'll see you later. I've got to go take a shower and get rid of some of this sweat." It was hard to read the expression on Brent's face, but he definitely didn't look happy.

"Yeah," he said. "Be careful, Julie."

Julie looked at him, saw the concern in his eyes, but didn't know what to say. "Yeah, okay." Then she walked away.

● ● ●

The party was already in full swing when Julie and Jennifer walked in. Again, Julie had just told her parents she was hanging out with the team tonight after the big win. She thought about the conversation she had had with her mom just before Jennifer picked her up.

"Is Brent going with you to the party tonight?"

"No, he's not. He has other plans."

"But I thought Friday night was your date night with Greg and Kelly."

"It usually is, Mom. But this is special. The win against Fulton was a big one."

Her mom had hesitated, and then continued.

"Julie, is there drinking at these parties?"

"Whatever gave you that idea, Mom?"

"Just hearing things."

"No," she had lied. "We just get together and hang out. You can trust me, Mom. I wouldn't ever do that."

Her mom had nodded and looked relieved. The guilt gnawed at Julie's stomach.

She wasn't left to her thoughts for very long. As soon as they walked into the room she heard congratulations ring out about her win that afternoon. It felt good to be the center of attention. Julie smiled, laughed, and called back to everyone. It was fun to belong in this crowd. She felt her doubts begin to melt away.

"Congratulations, Julie!"

Julie looked up as Marshall appeared at her side. "Thanks, Marshall. How has your week been?"

"Good." He looked deep into her eyes with a penetrating stare. "But I expect it to get better."

Julie blushed and looked down for an instant but then raised her eyes to meet his again. If she was going to be a part of this world she couldn't be a baby. She forced her brown eyes to meet his.

"Ready for something to drink?" He held out a beer.

"Thanks." Julie took it and tipped her head back to take a sip. It didn't taste nearly so bad this time. Tipping her head back further she took a longer draw. Lowering her can, she smiled into Marshall's eyes. She didn't understand the flash of triumph she saw in his eyes, but she recognized the obvious admiration.

Two beers later, Julie knew she wasn't going to stop. Carla's parents weren't home, so there weren't even any pretended limits that people were setting. She excused herself from Marshall and her other friends and went searching for Jennifer. She found her in a far corner with some friends. Julie was relieved that Jennifer lived just around the corner. At least they wouldn't be in a car.

"Jennifer, can I talk to you a minute?"

"Sure. What's up?"

Julie took a deep breath. She knew she wasn't on a good course, but she had no intention of backing out. "Do you think I could spend the night with you tonight?"

Jennifer studied her a moment and then shrugged. "Sure. My parents will be asleep when I get in. It won't make any difference." She looked like she was going to say something else, but didn't

"Thanks."

Julie headed for the phone. She needed to call her parents before she had any more to drink. She didn't want them to suspect anything. It was easy to get her mom's permission. She had just asked her to be home by lunch the next day Relieved, she returned to where Marshall was waiting for her. The first two beers were already working on her. She felt relaxed and happy. She reached eagerly for

the beer he held out to her. He laughed and pulled
her down on the sofa next to him. Julie found it
easy to laugh and talk as he held her close. This was
fun.

She didn't know how many beers she had consumed before Marshall pulled her into an embrace
that she didn't really like, but didn't have the
willpower to resist. Brent's face, his concerned eyes,
and his words, "be careful" flashed through her
mind, just as Marshall lowered his face to hers. Then
she lost track of time.

• • •

"What do we do?"

"I don't know that we can do anything, Kelly."
Greg was as concerned as she was about Julie.

"I just hope she's okay," Brent worried. "I know
what those parties can be like. She's out of her
league. Why in the world is she doing this?"

Kelly hesitated, not sure how much she should
say. Greg noticed the look on her face.

"What is it, Kelly?"

Kelly hesitated longer but finally offered, "She is
struggling with a lot of questions about God right
now. She's not sure where he fits in her life anymore . . . or if he even exists."

Greg and Brent stared at her.

Kelly continued. "She had a real tough time when
you tried to commit suicide, Brent. It raised a lot of
questions she can't find answers for. I think she's

just trying some new things because she's not sure the old ones work."

Brent groaned. "You mean my stupid mistake is hurting her, too?"

Kelly didn't know what to say. Silence filled the air for a few minutes as the boys thought about the information she had offered.

Greg broke the silence. "You're not responsible for her actions. What you did may have caused her to question, but it didn't make her decide to jump into the party scene and reject church and her Christian friends. That's a decision she made on her own."

Brent pondered his words. "What do we do now?"

"I don't know," Greg admitted. "Part of me wants to go into that party and drag her out. I know that won't do any good, though."

Kelly nodded. "I've thought the same thing. Sometimes I get angry over what she's doing, but then I try to remember she's hurting and she's probably really confused. All I know to do is pray for her."

The boys nodded, but the looks on their faces showed clearly that they wished they could do more.

NINE

J ulie groaned as she squinted her eyes against the bright light streaming in through Jennifer's bedroom window.

"Finally waking up?"

Julie looked over to where Jennifer was standing next to her white wicker dresser. "What time is it?"

"About 10 o'clock. I just got up about 15 minutes ago. My parents will start yelling if I'm not up by 10:30 so I decided to avoid a scene."

Julie stared at her friend in confusion. "My head is killing me."

"I'm not surprised. You haven't learned to hold your liquor yet."

"Huh?"

Jennifer sat down on the side of the bed and looked at her friend with a strange mixture of sympathy and disappointment. "How much of last night do you remember?"

Julie forced her thoughts to focus. She remembered being at the party. "I can remember my fourth beer . . ." Her mind struggled to recapture the events of the night before. "After that . . ." She was horrified to realize she really didn't know what had happened. She was even more horrified when she realized the last thing she clearly remembered was Marshall handing her the fourth beer and then pulling her down beside him on the sofa. She groaned out loud. What had she done?

Jennifer interpreted the look on her face. "Don't worry. I got you out of there before Marshall got carried away. He didn't like it, but that was too bad. I'm not sure how he'll treat you at the next party."

Julie shrugged. That was the least of her concerns. What in the world was she doing? "Did you . . . did you have much trouble getting me here?"

Jennifer just laughed. "No. You're really a very happy drunk. I had a little trouble keeping you quiet while I was getting you to my bedroom. I knew my parents would have gone ballistic if they had heard us. I'd had too much to drink myself, but I was in much better condition than you."

Julie fell silent as her thoughts raced.

Jennifer continued. "Don't be so worried about it. You had fun, didn't you?" She paused. "At least the part you remember! It's no big deal. Everyone does it. You'll learn to hold your liquor better and it won't put you out every time." Then she got a serious look on her face. "I won't always be around to rescue you, Julie. You could have had some trouble with Marshall. He has a reputation for taking what he wants," she warned.

Julie shuddered and shook her head. "How do I get rid of this headache?"

"A shower should help some. There are some aspirin in the bathroom. Take a few of those. You'll be all right." Jennifer's voice was matter-of-fact. Obviously she had dealt with this before.

Just then Julie heard loud voices. She looked at Jennifer questioningly.

Jennifer gave her a rueful smile. "It's just my parents. They're going through their morning ritual in the kitchen. They fight all the time." She shrugged. "You get used to it." She rose from where she was sitting next to the bed. "I should go tell them we have company. That will put them on their good behavior for a while."

Julie watched her as she disappeared through the door and then fell back onto the bed with a groan. It wasn't just her head that was hurting. Her heart hurt. Her mind hurt. And whatever she was feeling these days in her spirit, it hurt. She knew she was making some dumb decisions. She couldn't believe she had gotten drunk. It had been weird enough for her to be drinking at all. But to have gotten drunk and not remember what had happened? To have to be rescued by Jennifer from Marshall? Julie felt tears burn her eyes. What if Jennifer hadn't brought her here? What might have happened? She had heard enough stories to realize that Marshall could have taken advantage of her and she couldn't have stopped him.

She forced herself to look at the situation honestly. Would it have been all Marshall's fault if something had happened? Sure he had no right to take advantage of her, but she knew it never would have gone as far as it had if she hadn't been drunk. Drunk! That word again! Julie could hardly believe she was applying it to herself. She had always looked down on people who drank. Had always felt sorry for them and thought they were really dumb. Now she was one of them. What was she going to do?

Just then her thoughts were interrupted by angry voices from what must be the kitchen.

"What time did you get home last night?" asked an angry female voice.

Julie guessed it was Jennifer's mom. It was echoed by what must have been her father.

"We've told you we don't want you out to all hours of the night."

Jennifer's voice was raised in the same angry tone. "I wasn't out until all hours of the night! What difference does it make to you anyway? You were asleep when I came in. I didn't bother you!"

"And what's the big deal of bringing someone home? You never asked us."

That was Jennifer's mom. Julie cringed at the trouble she had caused her friend. But what kind of people were her parents, anyway? Julie couldn't

imagine her parents ever making one of her friends
feel unwelcome in their home.

"Oh, what's the big deal, Mom? You don't care
what I do. Julie isn't causing you any trouble. She's
a good friend of mine. She'll be gone soon."

"Well, see that she is, young lady," her mother
barked. "She's probably like you, not worth anything. Is she a trouble maker like you? Honestly, I
don't know what I did to deserve this!"

Silence fell and then Julie heard footsteps moving
toward the room where she sat holding her breath.
Were Jennifer's parents coming to throw her out?
Then the voices continued.

"We didn't tell you you could leave this room!"

The footsteps continued down the hall.

"Have it your way, young lady! Your father and
I are going out this morning. You have to watch
your brother and sister until we get back."

That stopped the footsteps. "But I did that last
weekend!" Jennifer protested.

"And you'll do it again this weekend," her father
boomed. "You have to do something to make it
worth our paying for you to live here."

The footsteps resumed. Tears were streaming
down Jennifer's face when she walked into the
room. Julie stared at her in sympathy. She couldn't
even imagine having her parents talk to her that
way. Or, she talk to them that way.

Jennifer managed a slight smile. "Sorry you have
to see the tears." She shrugged. "At least I don't give

my parents the satisfaction. I learned to control my feelings a long time ago. But sometimes it really gets to me, you know?"

Julie struggled with what to say. "I'm sorry, Jennifer. I had no idea your relationship with your parents was like this. Has it always been this bad?"

Jennifer shrugged again. "Oh, it wasn't that bad this morning. At least there was just yelling. When Dad really loses his cool he belts me. Even that's not as bad as it used to be. I think they realize they've lost control of me now that I'm older. They just like to tell me how no good I am." The break in her voice belied the defiance in her voice. "I'm going to go take a shower. You mind if I go first?"

Julie shook her head and watched her friend disappear into the bathroom door off her room. Then she sank back onto the bed and stared out the window. The day was cloudy and looked like it would produce rain soon. It matched her mood perfectly. Her mind was full of her friend's pain. She wanted to help so much. But what did she have to offer? Julie thought back to the first week of tennis when she had had the chance to ask Jennifer on the ski retreat. She should have done it. Going to church would help her.

Julie stopped and thought about what she'd just said. Did she really believe that, or was it just habit to think God could help her with her problems? She dropped her head into her hands and rubbed it to ease the ache. All the questions she had been shov-

ing back poured forward to taunt her. The party last
night hadn't helped. She was still confused. She was
still searching for answers. All she had done was
get herself a massive headache, make trouble for
Jennifer, and possibly give herself a reputation with
Marshall. Would she ever find the answers to all her
questions? Would she ever believe and have faith in
God again?

In a moment of honesty she asked herself one
final question. Would she ever start looking for the
answers?

• • •

Julie relaxed back against the plush sofa pillows
and watched her brothers play ping-pong. It was
good to be home. She had gotten there shortly
before lunch. The hot shower and aspirin had done
their job. She was rid of the ache in her head, even
if the one in her heart was still there. It had been
good to get home to the warmth and love of her
family. They weren't perfect, but they loved each
other. After watching Jennifer's family in action
this morning it had become something she appreci-
ated even more.

Just then her mother called down the den stairs.
"It's for you, Julie. It's Kelly."

Julie reached slowly for the phone. She wasn't
sure she wanted to talk to Kelly. What if she had a
lot of questions?

"Hi, Kelly."

"Hi, Julie. How's it going? How was the team party last night?"

"Oh, it was great! We had a lot of fun. Just a lot of talking and stuff. You should have been there." Julie rolled her eyes at the ridiculousness of the last statement. She couldn't even imagine Kelly in a scene like that.

"Yeah," Kelly said half-heartedly. "Look, I was calling to see if you wanted to go horseback riding. Granddaddy said you could take Ralph out again. Want to go?"

"I don't think so, Kelly. I appreciate the invitation, but I'm really tired right now. Sitting around the house sounds pretty appealing to me." The idea of being on Ralph was appealing too, but she didn't want to be around Kelly right now. Her friend could read her too well. She would start to ask questions and Julie didn't feel like talking.

"Okay." Kelly hesitated, not sure if she should say anything else. "I guess I'll see you at church tomorrow."

"Sure, see you tomorrow."

Thirty minutes later the phone rang again. It was Brent.

"Hi, Julie."

"Hi, Brent." Julie forced warmth into her voice. Didn't her friends know she just wanted to be left alone for a while?

"Greg and I were thinking it would be fun to crash at Kelly's tonight and play some games or something. Maybe get a video. We already talked to her. We know you're tired, so we thought you might get into that. What do you think?"

Julie pictured Brent's gentle, handsome face regretfully. What was she going to do about him? Would he find out about Marshall and about her being drunk last night? She knew locker room talk revealed most things going on in the school. She shook her head. "I don't think so, Brent. I didn't tell Kelly this, but I'm really not feeling too well. I think I just want to stay home tonight. Thanks for the invitation, though. Listen I have to go. I hear my mom calling me."

When she hung up, her brother Matt was staring at her from next to the ping-pong table. "I didn't hear Mom calling."

Julie shrugged.

Chris broke in. "That's just an excuse to get off the phone. Brent probably knew it, too." Her brother looked at her in disgust. "Even freshmen hear stuff in the locker room, you know. Brent's a great guy. I can't believe you're ditching him for some party guy."

Julie gave him a withering look and marched upstairs. She couldn't even find peace at home. Throwing herself across her bed she stared broodingly out her window. What if Chris told her parents that she was partying? She seemed to be making more and more of a mess of things.

It was 5 o'clock when the phone rang again. Julie had passed the afternoon puttering in her room and playing at some homework she needed to catch up on. Her mother's voice floated up the staircase. "It's for you again, Julie."

What now? Julie reached for the phone next to her bed. "Hello."

"Hi, Julie. This is Jennifer."

Julie didn't even want to talk to her. It only reminded her of last night and all of her confusion. She just wanted to be home and escape from life a little while. "Hi, Jennifer."

"What are you doing tonight?"

Julie listened a little closer. "Are you crying, Jennifer?"

Jennifer gave a muffled laugh. "What would make you think that?" Silence. "Okay, maybe I am. Dad got home a little while ago. He must have met some of his buddies for a drink after he and Mom went out. Anyway, things got a little heated. I just want to get out of the house for a while."

"Are you okay, Jennifer?" Julie asked anxiously. "Oh, sure."

Her muffled tones indicated that was far from the truth. Julie wanted to stay at home, but she knew she needed to help her friend. After all, she had gotten her out of a tight spot the night before.

"I'll be over in about 20 minutes, Jennifer."

"Great! Hey, Sandy is having some people come over tonight. Why don't we go over. It's not a party or anything, no big deal. How about it?"

Julie rebelled at the idea but she couldn't bring

herself to say no. She had worked too hard to be accepted on the tennis team. "That sounds okay. See you soon."

Julie walked downstairs to tell her parents her plans.

Her mother cast her a curious look. "I thought you were tired and didn't want to go anywhere tonight."

Julie decided to opt for partial truth. "I am, Mom. But Jennifer is going through a tough time right now. She needs me."

Her mom nodded slowly. "Be home by 11. I don't want you to be too tired for church tomorrow."

• • •

The first hour or so at Sandy's had been fun. There were only six members of the team there. They had talked about tennis, listened to music, and played some pool. Julie was hoping this evening was going to be different. She didn't want to get drunk again. So far no alcohol had been brought out. Watching Jennifer, she was glad to see her talking and laughing. Her eyes had been swollen from crying when she had first picked her up, but she seemed to have put that behind her now.

"Anyone thirsty?" Sandy grinned as she held up four six-packs of beer. "This is all I could talk out of my parents. Seems one of their friends let their kids have a party at their home, and one of the kids left drunk and had a head-on collision going home. He's in the hospital pretty bashed up, but they say he's going to be fine. Anyway, my parents seemed to have gotten a little scared about buying booze for us. They'll get over it, though. They can't really say much, as much as they drink." Her voice grew defiant and then she smiled again. "There's 24 cans. We can each have four."

Julie shuddered. Her memories of what four cans of beer had done to her were too fresh. But she didn't refuse a can when Sandy passed it over to her. She would just take it easy. Besides, there was no way she was going to let her parents know what she was doing. They would be waiting up when she got home. She would be careful tonight.

It was only 10:30, but Julie was more than ready to go home. Everyone but her had drunk their quota of beer. They evidently could handle it better than she could. No one was horribly drunk, but they had all had too much to drink. Coarse language filled the air while Sandy described her night with Sam the night before.

Julie looked around slowly. This was so empty. There was no life here. All she saw were hurting people who were trying to cover up their pain with partying and alcohol. What was she doing here? Trying to cover up her own pain she guessed. She wasn't really any different from the rest. She was using alcohol to fit in . . . to drown out the questions that screamed through her mind when she was quiet long enough to think about them.

TEN

Julie was almost completely silent in the car on the way over to youth group. Kelly exchanged concerned glances with Brent and Greg, but they just kept talking about what had happened that weekend. They didn't want to make Julie feel any more uncomfortable.

Julie couldn't bring herself to do anymore than stare morosely out the window. The whole weekend had been horrible. The party Friday night, Jennifer's fight with her family, Chris knowing she was partying, the emptiness of last night. And now she was having to go to youth group. All she wanted to do was stay home and be alone. She had known better than to even mention it to her mother. Her mother hadn't had to force her to go to church in a long time. But Julie was pretty sure she would if she tried to stop going altogether. Julie was aware both of her parents were concerned about her.

Heaving a heavy sigh she realized they were

almost at the church. Wanting to be, or not, she was here. She would try to make the best of it. Zoning out had become pretty easy for her. It had been simple during this morning's service. She had sung the songs, but she had no idea what the sermon was about. Playing games was becoming a part of who she was. It was only for two hours. She could do it.

Julie almost groaned out loud when she walked in and saw the banners on the youth room wall. TEEN TALK SCENE! She had forgotten what night it was! If she had remembered she would have found some way to get out of being here, even if her parents had gotten upset. Once a month Martin designated Sunday night as TEEN TALK. They sang songs as usual, and had an activity, but he didn't do any talking. They all broke up into small groups of four to six people and talked about whatever topic was to be discussed that night. Before they did that, everyone had a chance to anonymously write questions concerning the topic. The questions were passed around and they all talked about them.

"Oh, good!" Kelly exclaimed. "TEEN TALK SCENE! I had forgotten what night it was. This is my favorite time of the month."

"You hate to hear me talk that much, huh?"

Kelly whirled around with a look of horror on her face until she saw Martin's wide grin. "Gosh, no, Martin! I love to hear you talk." Then she grinned slyly. "It's just that I like to hear us talk more!"

Julie smiled as the two bantered back and forth. TEEN TALK SCENE used to be her favorite time, too. It's just that she didn't feel like talking to anyone about her faith or what she believed right now. How could she when she didn't know herself?

"Hi, Julie." Martin walked forward to give her a big hug.

"Hi, Martin."

"We've been missing you on Wednesday nights." There was no condemnation or accusation in his tone. He was simply stating how he felt. "I understand tennis is keeping you pretty busy."

Julie managed to laugh lightly. Why did she have this sudden urge to start crying? "Yeah. It's pretty demanding. Things should lighten up when the season is over. It's fun, though."

"That's good."

Julie looked away from Martin's penetrating eyes. He knew her too well. She could sense he was looking for something. Could he tell that she wasn't okay? Grabbing Kelly's hand she laughed back over her shoulder. "We're going to go grab a seat. I'm not interested in the floor tonight." She could tell Kelly was surprised. Julie hadn't hardly spoken to her all night. But she allowed herself to be led over.

Forty-five minutes later, the singing and activity were over. Julie was pleased with how she had done. She had managed to laugh and talk and fit right in with everyone. It had become very important to her that Martin think she was all right. There had been times in the past when he had been concerned and cornered her to find out what was wrong. She didn't want that to happen. Her emotions were too raw. She didn't want to have to answer questions.

Martin stepped in front of everyone. "Everyone pull out the paper and pen I handed you a little while ago. Remember the rules of TEEN TALK. You don't have to actually write a question, but you have to write something . . . even if you just tell me the sky is blue. I don't want anyone to feel uncomfortable if they do have a question. Understand?" He waited until he saw nods around the room.

"Okay. You have three minutes to write your questions. The topic tonight is alcohol and teen drinking. You may begin."

Julie's head shot up and she stared at Martin. He was looking at her with an unreadable expression. Quickly she looked back down. She would have been perfectly happy if the floor had opened to swallow her just then. All she wanted to do was jump up and run from the room. That wouldn't do any good, though. Fighting panic, she chewed her lip and stared fixedly at her sheet of paper. "Write anything," he had said. Picking up her pen, she wrote slowly, "The sky is very blue. The grass is very green. Why are you so mean?" When she was done, she slowly folded the paper and held it. It wouldn't do any good to panic. She would make it through this. Then she would have to figure out more excuses to stay home from youth group. She had an idea she wasn't going to be feeling too well next week.

"Okay, everyone. Pass up your sheets of paper. Janie and I have arranged the chairs into groups of five tonight. One at a time I want you to come up here and pick a slip of paper from the bag. Go over to the group of chairs that has the corresponding color of your paper. We'll shuffle the questions and bring them around to you."

Julie walked forward slowly with everyone else. She hoped she wouldn't be in the same group as Kelly, Greg, or Brent. They knew her too well. She wasn't that lucky. Turning toward her group of chairs, she saw Kelly pulling a chair out. She thought about changing colors with someone but didn't want to be so obvious. Slowly she headed toward her group.

Matt, a senior at the only private school in town, read the first question.

"Where do kids get alcohol? I thought it was really hard to get, but I have friends who don't have any trouble."

Kelly spoke first. "I have some friends who get their alcohol from their parents' liquor cabinet. Lots of them get drunk the first time that way."

"Yeah," agreed Kathy. "Parents throw a fit when their kids drink. But they do it themselves. It's kind of hard to hear them say not to do it when they do it. I've got a lot of friends who got their first drink from their parents' supply."

"It's no big deal for kids to get alcohol," said Scott, a junior at Kingsport. "There are parties around town every weekend. My friends tell me that college guys over 21 take money from them, go buy the alcohol, and bring it in. There are even a couple of stores here that don't bother to card. You can just go in and get it."

"Or, parents buy it for the kids." This from Alec, a Kingsport sophomore. "I got invited to a party this past Friday, but I didn't go. The girl's parents buy the beer for everyone because they figure they're going to drink anyway. They prefer to have them at home."

Julie thought about Sandy. That's how her parents felt. She also remembered the story of Sandy's parents' friends. Obviously, she wasn't the only one who had heard that story.

"Yeah. Did y'all hear about Jason?" Matt asked. "He went to one of those parties a couple of weeks ago. The girl's parents had bought a lot of alcohol for them. Of course, they tell everyone not to drink and then drive, but who is listening? What happens, happens. Anyway, Jason got really loaded and then drove home. He lost control on one of the curves on River Road. Ran head-on into a pickup truck. The other driver is okay, but Jason is pretty broken up. He'll be okay, but he's going to be in the hospital for a while."

Julie thought about her first party. If Jennifer hadn't had to babysit the next morning, she knew her friend would have gotten drunk. Julie rode home with her that night. The same thing could have happened to her. She saw her friends leaving the parties. Very few of them had any business being behind the wheel of a car.

They talked for a few more minutes and then Matt read the next question.

Why do kids drink?

Matt chuckled. "Boy, that's the hundred-dollar question."

Julie was glad it had been asked, though. She had some ideas but she wanted to hear what everyone else had to say.

Matt sobered. "All I can tell you is why I drank."

Julie looked at him in surprise. She didn't know very much about Matt. He had started coming to youth group in the past year, but since they didn't go to the same school she didn't see much of him. Had he had a drinking problem? His next words surprised her.

"I was on my way to having a bad drinking problem. I probably already had one, but I just didn't acknowledge it. I started drinking when I was 14. It was weird. I had always said I would never drink. I thought it was really stupid. I was an athlete. I wasn't going to mess up my body and my life." He paused. "When I got into high school things changed. I made the football team and I wanted to be a part of the gang. I said no the first few times, but then I got tired of being different. I just wanted to fit in. I started drinking just a little bit. Gradually it got to be a lot more. I only drank on the weekends, but I got drunk everytime. I wanted to stop but I just couldn't. Things at home weren't helping any. My dad was gone most of the time and me and my mom fought about everything. I'd get mad, go to a party, and drink to forget my anger." His face darkened as he relived that time in his life. "Anyway, it took something big to turn me around . . ."

Julie couldn't believe what she was hearing. And he was being so honest about it!

Matt continued. "One night, about a year-and-a-half ago, I had gone to a party at a friend's house. It was after the big homecoming game at my school. There were a lot of people there, some who weren't really drinkers, so I felt like a hot shot by showing how much I could drink. I really put it away that night. I don't remember much of what happened. The next morning when I woke up I was told I'd been in an accident the night before. My best friend was killed, but I hadn't even been scratched. My friend had been drinking and wrapped the car around a pole." Tears filled his eyes at the memory.

Silence gripped the group as he talked.

"I was so sure it would never happen to me. Or at least not to someone I cared about. It didn't seem real until I saw his body in the casket at the funeral. Then I fell apart. I felt like it was my fault." He took a deep breath. "Anyway, two days later my parents took me out of school and put me in a drug rehab program. I hated them for it, but it was the best thing they could have done. I fought it for a while, but finally I gave my life to Christ and things began to turn around. I haven't had a drink in almost a year. I still go to Alcoholics Anonymous meetings twice a week. My family went through a lot of counseling and things are much better there. We all learned a lot. I especially learned how precious life is. I'll never forget Jimmy. It still hurts when I think about him, but the Lord is helping me with it."

Matt's voice drifted into silence.

Kelly broke the quiet after several moments. "Wow. I had no idea you had been through all that."

Matt just nodded.

Martin had walked up behind them as Matt was talking. He laid his hand on the boy's shoulder and squeezed it gently. "Sharing all that took a lot of courage, Matt. I'm proud of you."

Matt shrugged. "I knew I would have to tell it sometime. When you mentioned the topic for tonight, I had a feeling now was the time. It feels kind of good to get it out."

"Thanks for telling us, Matt," Julie said softly. Only she knew how hard it had hit her.

"Yeah. Thanks, Matt," Kathy added. "I must admit there have been times when I wanted to drink. Most of the time it's no big deal because I have so many Christian friends, but I've had some people pressure me to try it. Sometimes I'm just curious to find out what it's like. But I don't want to get hooked on it. I guess I'm kind of scared."

Matt grinned at her. "That kind of fear can be a good thing. I wish I'd been more afraid. It would have kept me out of a lot of trouble."

"Do your friends at school pressure you now to drink?"

Matt shook his head. "They tried a little at first. They don't anymore. They know how I feel about it. The sad thing is that so many of them are still drinking . . . even after Jimmy died. It's like they don't want to think about it. They just keep drinking. I learned something at the rehab center. It's not bad to be different. It takes a lot more courage to be different than to just swim along with the rest of the crowd. My counselor told me that any dead fish can float with the current, but only a live, fighting fish can swim against it. I decided I didn't want to be a dead fish. I wanted to do something with my life. I didn't just want to be part of a crowd drifting into emptiness."

Julie recalled her impression of the emptiness she had seen last night. Did she want to just go along with the crowd . . . or dare to be different?

Matt had one last thing to say. "Some of the kids at school hassle me about drinking, but I've come to realize it's because they're jealous. They actually respect me for taking a stand. They just wish they could do it."

Julie thought of the disappointment she had seen

on Jennifer's face when she had jumped into the party and drinking scene. Had she hoped Julie would be different? Thoughts jumbled in her brain as she sought to sort them through.

"Okay, gang. We've run out of time. Let's all close in prayer and call it a night." Martin led the group in prayer and then Julie walked slowly out to Kelly's car.

Julie and Kelly were alone in the car. Kelly had dropped the guys off and was now headed toward Julie's house. Julie suspected she was being set up for a talk. It would have been easier for Kelly to have taken her home before Brent. She waited quietly. She didn't have to wait for long.

"Julie . . . I'm not . . . sure how to . . . say this."

Julie wanted to tell her not to bother, but she remained silent.

Kelly forged on, obviously struggling with her words. "I'm really concerned about you, Julie. Do you want to talk about anything?"

Julie could feel her defenses rising. "No."

Kelly absorbed her simple response. Then she turned her head to look at her friend. "What's going on, Julie? Somebody called me today. Said they had seen you at the party on Friday night. That you were in pretty bad shape." She didn't add what they had said about her being with Marshall.

"It sounds to me like your friend needs to mind her own business," Julie said tightly.

"She's just concerned, Julie. We all are."

"There's no reason to be concerned. I'm fine. I'm

just hanging out at some parties, that's all."

Kelly decided a more direct approach was needed. "My friend also told me how Jennifer saved you from Marshall."

Julie's temper flared. "I'd appreciate it if everyone would quit talking about me. It's my life! I'll live it the way I want to."

"But . . ."

Julie didn't want to hear anymore. "Just leave me alone, Kelly! I don't need you, or anyone else, to try and control my life. I'm going to make my own decisions. And don't throw any of that Christian stuff in my face. I'm tired of hearing about it. I don't know what I believe anymore. I don't know if I believe anything! I'm trying to figure it all out. I don't need a bunch of people pressuring me." Her voice rose in a shout as she flung out the ugly words. Looking up she realized they were at a stop sign only a block from her house. She grabbed the car doorhandle, threw open the door, and jumped out. "I'll walk home the rest of the way." Then she turned away and started to stride angrily down the road.

• • •

Julie's parents had been watching TV in the den when she had gotten home. She had called to them to let them know she was there and had escaped to her room. Now she lay face down on her bed, staring out the window.

Tears streamed down her cheeks.

ELEVEN

Kelly walked over and laid her tray down next to Greg's. "Where's Julie, Brent?" She had not had a chance to talk to the boys about the blowup with Julie the night before. She had been crying when she walked into her house. Two hours of talking with her parents had helped, but she was still unsure what to say to her friend.

"I don't think she'll be joining us today," Brent said quietly. "I don't know if she will again, period."

Kelly looked at him. His voice was quiet but sounded definite.

Brent answered the question in her eyes. "Julie called me last night and broke up."

"Oh." Then, "I'm really sorry, Brent."

Brent shrugged. "That's the way it goes sometimes."

"What happened?" Kelly asked. It was obvious Greg and Brent had already talked, but she wanted to know, too.

"Oh, the usual line. She said she really liked me

136

and wanted to keep being good friends, but she just didn't think a steady relationship was a good idea right now. Said she had a lot going on and needed her freedom."

"What did you say?"

"What could I say? I'm surprised she didn't do it before now. I knew it was coming. I tried to get her to explain more, but she wouldn't answer any of my questions. Just told me she'd talk to me later and hung up."

Kelly didn't know what to say. Just then she saw Julie leave the line with a full tray. Julie looked over and caught her eye but lowered her eyes quickly and walked directly to the table where the tennis team was gathered. They welcomed her loudly and soon Julie was laughing and talking with the rest.

Kelly turned back to Brent. "Are you mad?"

"No," he said slowly and thoughtfully. "At least I'm not now. I guess I was at first, but then I prayed about it and spent a lot of time thinking last night. I know Julie is really hurting right now. She's making some dumb decisions but no dumber than the one I made when I tried to kill myself. My actions then are part of her problem now."

"She stood by me. It's the least I can do for her. I think Julie is a great girl. If I got mad at her for making some bad decisions I think I would be the world's worst hypocrite."

"Yeah," Kelly agreed. "I kind of came to the same conclusion last night." Briefly she told them about her encounter with Julie. Both of them whistled and shook their heads when she told how Julie had jumped out of the car and taken off.

"What did you do?" Greg asked.

It was Kelly's turn to shrug and ask, "What could I do? I didn't want to make her any madder and I knew I couldn't force her to talk to me. So, I just watched from a distance to make sure she got home okay and then I went home. I spent a lot of time talking to Dad and Peggy last night. I was pretty upset when I got home."

Greg nodded. "Did talking to them help?"

"Yeah. It really did. I was scared for Julie, but I was also angry. I mean, we've been such good friends. I couldn't believe she would yell at me like that. Especially when I was just trying to tell her I was concerned. Dad said she was probably scared herself and didn't know what she was doing. Peggy agreed. She said she went through a time when she was really questioning her faith and a lot of things in her life. She said she made a number of bad decisions, but she was just so confused she didn't know what end was up."

Kelly glanced over to where Julie was still laughing with her teammates. "Then she said something really interesting. She said sometimes it's hard to have always been a Christian. To have grown up in a Christian home. She's really glad she did, but she said that at some point she had to stop believing just because her parents did and because the church told her to. She had to decide if her faith was her own or not. She kind of envies her friends who met Christ later in life because they were a lot more mature when they made their decision. Once they had made it, it was there for good. She said she went through a hard time when she started asking a lot of questions."

Greg and Brent nodded thoughtfully.

Greg said, "That's one thing I really liked about my youth director back in Texas before I moved here. He let us ask a lot of questions. Any question we wanted to. He didn't always know the answer, but we would look for it together. I've talked to some people who have been made to feel like a heathen if they dare to ask questions. I have a feeling Martin is like my old youth director. It's too bad Julie won't go talk to him."

Kelly shook her head. "I don't think Julie is interested in talking to anyone right now."

"That's for sure," Brent agreed. "What did your parents think we should do?"

"Keep loving her. Look for ways to show her we care. Peggy thinks Julie will realize what she's doing and need us there to support her as friends. If we react to her the way she is to us, we'll shut those doors." Kelly paused. "Dad said it was a good lesson in loving unconditionally. It made me think about how horrible I was to Peggy when she first married Dad. She loved me that way. I guess the least I can do is to do that for Julie."

"I think your folks are right, Kelly," Greg said.
"Trying to force Julie to talk or trying to make her
feel bad about what she's doing will only drive her
further away. I guess we'll just have to take things
one day at a time."

• • •

Julie was exhausted when she walked onto the
court that afternoon. She didn't know how in the
world she was going to play a complete match.
Thank goodness the girl from Stanton High wasn't
supposed to be that good. She knew she could never
have repeated her performance of last week. Sleep
had been simply wishful thinking last night. Her
conversations with Kelly and Brent had drained her
emotionally, but her mind wouldn't quit replaying
them over and over.

She had wanted to cry when she walked by her
three friends in the cafeteria that day. Part of her
wanted to have things be the same old way. Another
part of her said all that was over and she just needed
to let it go. She had done too much to have the same
friendship they had had before. She had formed new
friendships with people on the tennis team. If she
longed for the old days, she just needed to remember she had made the decision to do whatever it
took to fit in.

"Are you okay, Julie?" Coach Crompton had
walked up and was regarding her with a worried
look. "You look terrible!"

Julie forced a smile. "I'm okay, Coach. I'm just really tired. I didn't get much sleep last night. I'll be fine once I get playing." She gave a feeble laugh. "Once the competitive juices start flowing, I'll forget all about being tired."

Her coach nodded but still looked concerned.

Julie took a deep breath and resolved to play her best. She didn't want to let her coach down. A few minutes later the whistle blew to indicate play.

"You can do it, Julie!"

"Go get 'em, Julie!"

At the sound of the voices, Julie looked sharply toward the stands. What in the world were Brent and the rest doing here? She had been so horrible to them last night. Yet there they were, cheering her on like nothing had happened. Julie swallowed hard and blinked away the tears burning her eyes. She had to play tennis. Turning back to her opponent, she got ready to receive her serve.

Julie had to play hard but nothing like she had played the week before. She was pretty sure the match would have been even easier if she hadn't been so tired. But at the end of 45 minutes she had managed to win the match five to three. She was glad it was over, but she didn't feel the flush of victory she had felt last week. The glow seemed to be diminishing from everything. What was wrong with her? She was number two on the tennis team and was undefeated so far. It just didn't seem to matter much.

"Good job, Julie!"

"Thanks, Jennifer. How did your match go?"

"I lost," Jennifer said, shrugging her shoulders. "I just couldn't seem to focus today."

"Yeah. I know what you mean. It was a good thing this girl wasn't as good as Sarah last week. I would have been demolished."

Julie was walking out the gate when she heard her name being called. She turned around to see Kelly behind her. She probably wanted to blast her about how she had treated her last night. Julie braced herself.

"Want to go out for some ice cream?" Kelly asked.

Julie stared at her. She just wanted to ask her out for ice cream? She wasn't going to tell her what an idiot she was? She was so surprised she didn't know what to say for a few moments. Opening her mouth to say yes, she was aware of Carla and Sandy walking toward her. Snapping her lips closed, she looked at Kelly coolly.

"No thanks. I have plans." Turning, she walked away. Once again she struggled with tears blurring her vision.

Jennifer hadn't said anything about the tense exchange. That was until they were headed into the locker room. "Kelly seems really nice."

Julie shrugged, hating herself even before she spoke the words. "She's okay, I guess. She can really get on my nerves sometimes." She was glad Kelly wasn't there to hear her hateful words.

Jennifer gave her a curious glance and turned away to get stuff out of her locker.

Julie was tired. She just wanted to take a shower and go home. Just then Coach Crompton walked in to tell them what a good job they had done. So far the team was undefeated. Julie wished she could be more excited about it. Once the coach was gone, she climbed wearily into the shower and let the hot water wash the sweat from her body. She would be home soon and then she could relax. At least she didn't have to worry about a party tonight. It was Monday. Everyone had to be at home.

"Look what I've got, team! I smuggled it in in my bag."

Julie turned to where Carla was standing next to her locker. Speaking in a triumphant tone, she was holding up a large bottle of wine. Julie groaned to herself. She didn't want to drink today. She just wanted to be alone.

Carla, grinning, continued. "I think our winners should get the first swigs."

Julie watched as Sandy took it from her and downed a large gulp. What if the coach walked in now? They would all be goners. Probably suspended from school. She didn't want anything to do with this. Turning away she started pulling things from her locker.

"Your turn, Julie."

Julie turned slowly. "No thanks, Carla. I don't feel like it today."

She was surprised at the anger that flashed in Carla's eyes. "What's wrong? Are you getting too good for us? I thought you were part of the team. It's tradition to celebrate wins." Carla's eyes narrowed. "Or are you hooking back up with your goody-two-shoes Christian friends? I saw them at the match today."

Julie wanted to take her words and shove them back down her throat. She hated herself as she reached for the bottle. Tossing her head back she gulped a huge swallow. Trying to ignore the burning in her throat she gazed at Carla levelly as she handed back the bottle. Saying nothing, she turned around, gathered the things out of her locker, and walked out of the locker room.

Silence followed her.

TWELVE

J ulie breathed a sigh of relief when practice ended on Wednesday. She knew she wasn't playing good tennis. She would be in trouble at the match on Friday if she wasn't able to pull it together. Picking up her towel and racquet cover, she headed for the locker room. At least no one had said anymore about Monday afternoon. It was like they wanted to pretend it hadn't happened. That was just fine with her.

"Hey, Julie. You want to stay longer today? My body sure could use that Jacuzzi."

"I don't think so, Jennifer. I've got a lot of homework to do. I told my mom I would be home early tonight." She hadn't told her mom anything, and she didn't have a lot of homework. She just didn't have the heart to play tennis anymore.

"Julie, can I talk to you for a minute?"

Julie turned at the sound of her coach's quiet voice. Uh oh, she was probably going to get a lecture about how lousy she was playing. Well, she deserved it. "Sure, Coach."

She followed Coach Crompton over to an empty bench. She watched as the rest of the team filed into the locker room, some of them casting glances in her direction. She hoped everyone was gone by the time she got in there. She didn't feel like answering their questions. The serious look on her coach's face told her this wasn't going to be a pleasant conversation.

"I'm concerned about how you're playing, Julie."

Julie just lowered her head and nodded.

"What's going on? You're not the same girl that showed up for tryouts five weeks ago. Is something wrong?"

Julie could handle being yelled at. She couldn't handle this nice approach. She battled the tears choking her throat. She couldn't have said anything if she wanted to.

She heard Coach Crompton give a deep sigh. "I can't help you if you won't talk to me." Silence. Then, "Okay, let me know if there is anything I can do. But I have to be honest with you. The number two position on the team is an important one. You worked hard to earn it, and you're going to have to work hard to keep it. If you're playing doesn't improve, I'm going to have to move you down on the list."

Julie raised her head in protest and spoke her first words. "But I won Monday!"

"Yes," Coach Crompton agreed, "but your heart wasn't in it. The girl from Stanton isn't that good.

A lot of players on our team could have beaten her. You aren't going to be playing any more girls like that. The rest of the teams we're going to meet are tough. I owe it to the team to put the best players possible in each position." She paused and her voice softened, "I know something is bothering you, Julie. I can see it in your eyes. If you can't talk to me, at least find *someone* to talk to. Whatever is bothering you can probably be worked out."

Julie just nodded. They sat in silence for a few minutes.

"Anyway, I'm going to let you stay in the number two position for this Friday's match. We leave for Florida Sunday afternoon. We'll be doing a lot of playing down there. Maybe that will help you. You can go take your shower now. I'll see you tomorrow."

"Thanks, Coach," Julie managed. She was miserable. The sting of the shower did nothing to improve her mood. She was messing everything up. When in the world was this going to stop? What should she do? Coach Crompton had suggested she find someone to talk to. Maybe that was what she needed to do. She just didn't know who. Unbidden, Martin's face floated into her mind. She pushed it back out. He would probably just preach at her. She sure didn't want to hear that.

Stepping out of the shower she began to towel off.

"Is everything okay?" Jennifer appeared in front

of her, already dressed and ready to leave.

Julie shrugged. "Yeah. Coach Crompton just wanted to tell me I'm playing lousy tennis. I already knew that. She didn't have to tell me."

"I'm sorry, Julie."

Julie looked quickly at her friend. The sincerity in her voice was real. The caring in her eyes was, too. "Thanks, Jennifer. It'll get better. I just have a lot on my mind."

"Yeah, I know what you mean." Jennifer turned to leave and then swung back.

Julie was stunned by her next comment.

"Maybe you need to go to church tonight."

Julie just stared at her. Jennifer gave her a quick smile, turned, and left.

The locker room was empty as Julie slipped into her navy blue warmup and dried her hair. Her mind was working furiously. She couldn't believe Jennifer had suggested she go to church. Where in the world had that come from?

The trip to Florida was like a lifeline being thrown out to her. She could hardly wait to get away from everything and everyone here in Kingsport. If she had really thought about it, she would have realized she was taking the source of most of her problems with her . . . the team, her questions, and the reality of alcohol. All she could think of was that she was getting away. Surely that was all she needed to pull it all together.

●　●　●

"You're home early tonight, dear."

Julie swung her duffle bag onto the kitchen table and sniffed appreciatively. Mom had fixed fried chicken and mashed potatoes for dinner. Reaching over she grabbed some grapes off the kitchen counter and stuffed them in her mouth. "Yeah. I decided I wasn't in the mood for an extra hour of tennis today."

Her mother just nodded and turned back to the stove to turn the chicken. Julie sank down in a chair and looked around at the coziness of her home. The peace was like a balm to her soul. She saw her mom turn and look at her curiously but she didn't say anything. Julie was thankful she was leaving her alone. The silence pervading the room stretched into almost 20 minutes. Still, Julie just sat there.

Finally her mom broke the silence. "Are you planning on going to church tonight?" Her voice was deliberately casual.

Julie opened her mouth to say no. "Yeah, I'm planning on going."

"I'm glad," her mother said simply. "Dinner will be ready in about ten minutes."

Julie retreated to her bedroom to change. What had prompted her to say yes? Now she was committed, and she couldn't come up with a real reason to change her mind. Besides, there was a small part of her that wanted to be there. She didn't understand it, but she would go. Rifling through her closet, she chose some blue corduroy slacks and a long, cream-colored sweater. A little dab of mascara was all the makeup she wanted. Ten minutes later she slipped into her chair at the table.

• • •

Everyone at youth group had been surprised and pleased to see Julie there. No one was more surprised than Kelly, Greg, and Brent. But they didn't say anything other than how glad they were to see her.

Martin made a few announcements and then jumped right into his topic for the evening. "Tonight we are going to look at people in the Bible who asked questions."

Julie's head shot up at his words, but no one seemed to notice her. Hurriedly she lowered her head to hide the flush on her cheeks. Had Martin picked this subject just because she was going to be here? But that wasn't possible. She hadn't been to Bible Study in almost a month. He had no way of knowing she was coming. This should be interesting.

Martin continued. "Let's take a look at Moses first. His story is here in Exodus. Let's start in Chapter 2." He waited patiently while pages were flipped to the proper place. "I'm going to give a very brief rundown. Moses was born during a time when the Egyptian pharoah had commanded that all male Israeli babies be killed at birth. His mother just couldn't do that, so she made a little reed basket, put him in it, and set in on the river, hoping someone would find it. Someone did. The pharoah's daughter. She saved Moses' life, and he came to live in the palace and have the best of everything.

"When he was 40, he was trying to help some of his fellow Israelites and killed an Egyptian. He thought his fellow men would appreciate what he had done. He was wrong. To escape the situation he ran away and spent 40 years in virtual seclusion. Then God appeared to him in a burning bush and told him to go back to Egypt and save his people."

Here Martin paused and smiled. "Now, I don't know about you, but if God spoke to me in a burning bush I think I would be so awestruck I would do whatever he said! Not Moses. He started arguing with God. He started asking questions about why he had to do this thing. Couldn't God find someone else? Now, God had gone to a lot of trouble to use a burning bush to make sure Moses knew it was him. And here Moses was asking him questions. If I were God, I think I would have blasted him. God used him anyway. It was Moses who led all of Israel out of Egypt after God used him to perform many miracles before the Pharoah." Martin started flipping pages again. "There's a lot more to that story, but we don't have all night."

Finding what he was looking for he said, "Turn to Psalm 22 and look at the first verse." Martin waited and then looked at Kelly. "Kelly, would you read it please?"

Kelly nodded, "My God, my God, why have you forsaken me? Why are you so far from saving me, so far from the words of my groaning?"

Julie could definitely relate with David.

Martin smiled. "David is asking some pretty tough questions there. Ones that I think all of us, at some time in our lives, will ask. Let's take a look at David, though. Where had he come from? He had been a lowly shepherd boy until God used him to destroy the huge Philistine with just a slingshot and a few stones. Then he saved him when King Saul was trying to kill him. God went to a lot of trouble to make sure David was king of Israel. And still David was asking God why he had forsaken him?" Martin laughed. "Don't you think God must shake his head and wonder when we're ever going to get it?"

"Let's look at one more . . . Jesus. Even he asked questions of God. The one that stands out most in my mind is the one he asked when he was hanging on the cross, close to death. He asked the very same question David did, 'My God, my God, why have you forsaken me?'" Martin fixed them all with a steady gaze. "Now get this picture. Jesus was the Son of God. He knew the Father! He had lived on earth for 33 years doing unbelieveable miracles and seeing God constantly at work. He had told all of his followers this was going to happen. Had said he would be dead for three days and then come back to life. And yet, here he was at the end, crying out to God with questions."

Silence filled the room as Martin spoke.

"Do you think God was angry with his question?" Martin's voice was deliberate as he answered his own question. "I don't think He was. I think he understood exactly. I think he understood when Moses asked questions. And when David asked questions. God made humans. He knows how the human mind and spirit work." Martin paused again. "I'll go even further than that. I think God wants us to ask questions. He is not threatened when we question him and look for answers. That's the only way we are ever able to truly believe.

"But I think I need to add something to that. So many people like to ask questions just for the sake of asking questions. Especially when it comes to faith in Christ. It's not something they really want to deal with so they throw up walls by asking questions. They don't want answers. They just want to seem to have a good argument for not believing. My challenge to you is to ask questions. But don't just ask them for the sake of asking. Ask, and then look for answers. Some questions you'll have for a long time. Some you'll never find solid answers for. I still don't know why my father had to die when I was 19 years old. We had just developed a good relationship and I was looking forward to the years ahead. I don't know why, but I have learned to trust that God knows what He's doing." Then Martin smiled. "But a lot of questions you will find answers for. God wants to help you understand. He wants to help you dig for truth so that when you find it, it will be your own. It will be something you can hang on to."

Kelly raised her hand.

"Yes, Kelly?" Martin asked.

"My stepmother, Peggy, said something the other night I thought was really interesting. She said that sometimes being raised in a Christian home all your life can be really tough. That as you get older you start questioning everything you ever believed and that it can be hard to find answers."

Martin nodded. "Peggy is absolutely right. It used to be that most kids didn't start questioning their faith and what they had been taught until they were in college. Now it seems to be happening younger and younger. I would hazard a guess that some of you are asking questions right now. That makes it tough because you're still developing your ability to think through things and all the questions end up making you very confused. But that doesn't change the fact that you're asking them. My advice is to not be afraid of asking. Just make sure they're honest questions . . . ones you really want answers for. Then look for the answers. God will meet you. He wants you to know him. He wants you to be able to claim your faith as your own."

Martin glanced down at his watch. "I want to do one more thing before we end tonight. I'd like to give each of you a slip of paper and a pen. On that paper I want you to write the one question that is bugging you the most. Then I want you to put it in your Bible. You'll find it again a few months from now. You can decide then if you've gotten your answer, if you're honestly looking, or if it's just an excuse to not believe."

Silence pervaded the room as he passed out paper and pen and heads bent to write.

Julie sat silently for a few minutes. Martin's words were ringing in her mind. Finally she wrote, How can I know God is real? Folding it, she slipped it in her Bible.

● ● ●

Martin's words had hit Julie hard. She knew she had a lot to think about. She was still sitting on the floor against the sofa when Kelly approached her.

"Would you like to go get some ice cream tonight?"

Julie looked up at her, grateful for the warmth she saw in her friend's eyes. "Yeah. That sounds like fun. I need to call my mom first. She's supposed to pick me up in about 15 minutes. She needed the car tonight."

"Okay," Kelly replied. "I'll be happy to drop you off after we eat."

"Thanks, Kelly. I appreciate that." She started to walk off but then hesitant, she turned back. "Are the guys going, too?"

It was Kelly's turn to hesitate. "How would you feel about them going?"

Julie was sure that had been the original plan. She
wasn't sure how she felt about spending time with
Brent. They hadn't seen each other or talked since
she had broken up with him.

Kelly waited patiently for her answer.

Julie thought quickly. She had told Brent she still
wanted to be friends. Couldn't they just go as
friends? She realized that she wanted very much to
spend time with her friends. She had missed them.
She could walk away again or she could try and
rebuild the friendship. She nodded, "I'd like that."

She couldn't help noticing Kelly's look of relief.
It hit Julie that it had probably been hard for Kelly
to ask her. After all, she had been terribly rude to
her friend the last couple of times they had talked.

"Kelly?"

"Yeah?"

"Thanks for the invitation."

Kelly smiled. "I'm just glad you're going."

"Yeah. Me too."

Twenty minutes later the four of them were
seated in their favorite booth at Friendly's Ice
Cream. The place was almost empty. All of them
gave their orders and then settled back into the big
vinyl seats.

"You leave for Florida on Sunday don't you,
Kelly?" Greg asked.

Julie nodded. "About 6 o'clock at night. The
coach's husband is going to drive the van. He
prefers to drive all night. Says the traffic is much

better so they get there faster. That's fine with me. I'm planning on sleeping the whole way."

"Is the whole team going?"

Julie looked at Brent as he asked the question. He was being wonderful. He wasn't acting awkward and he was being genuinely friendly toward her. Julie smiled at him warmly and was rewarded by a quick smile and a flash in his eyes. "Yeah. Everybody is going to be able to make it this year."

"I bet you can hardly wait!" Kelly exclaimed. "I would love to be going to Florida for Spring Break. I'm so tired of cold weather. I want warmth and sunshine."

"And seven months from now you'll be groaning for 'sweater days' and cold weather," Julie laughed.

"True. But that's then and this is now. Now I want to be warm and have a suntan."

"It *will* be nice to come back and show off my suntan. I love to make people jealous!"

They bantered and laughed until their food was set down before them. As Julie dug into her brownie sundae she thought silently of her doubts about the trip. She really wanted to quit drinking. She didn't like what it did to her and she didn't like what it made her do. But how was she going to fit in with the team if she didn't? They were going to have chaperones, but she knew Carla and Sandy. They would figure out some way to get alcohol. What would she do when they did?

THIRTEEN

J ulie had been wide awake since 6 o'clock that morning. She had soaked in the beauty of coastal Georgia as she watched the sun rise. The low lying mist over the marshy lowlands spoke of a mystique that entranced her. White herons, and the occassional large blue heron she heard honking as it took off on long wings, were birds she had never seen.

She had cheered and urged Mr. Crompton to honk the horn as they passed the state sign saying "Welcome to Florida" as they sped down Interstate 95. Jennifer had woken up about 8 o'clock and was now eagerly absorbing the sights with her. They were just now passing through the horse country around Ocala. Julie thought how thrilled Kelly would be to see the endless pastures surrounded by gleaming white fences and full of beautiful, leggy thoroughbreds. The two girls laughed at the antics of the new foals prancing and playing in the emerald green fields.

Mr. Crompton had asked them to call him Mike. Julie turned to him eagerly. "Mike . . ."

"Don't say it, Julie," he warned with a grin. "I told you if I heard 'How long before we're there?' one more time I was going to make you walk. I really don't think you want to walk that far."

Julie laughed along with him, but he could tell she still wanted to ask the question.

Leaning down, Mike grabbed a map off the floorboard. "Here. Figure out where we are on the map. Then you can figure out how much longer it is till we get there."

"Great idea!" exclaimed Julie. Within seconds she and Jennifer were poring over the map, discussing locations and mileage.

Mike rolled his eyes at his wife. "That was easy enough. Why didn't I think of that about ten hours ago?"

"Hey, Mike, how much further is it?" This from a sleepy Jewel who had just woken up.

"Ask Julie. She's in charge of the map."

Julie spoke in a very important person voice. "According to my calculations, we should be at Sanibel Island in about three hours.

Mike stifled a chuckle.

"Yeah, well do you think we could stop making good time long enough to make a pit-stop?" Carla called from the back of the van.

Coach Crompton laughed. "I knew that would be coming soon. But it's been almost four hours since our last real stop. I'd say that's pretty good."

Her husband nodded and then pulled off at the fast approaching exit. "This is as good a place as any. I suppose we can let them terrorize McDonald's. They can even get something to eat." The car following him pulled into the parking lot right beside him. Sandy, Laura, and Amy jumped out and ran toward the bathroom.

"They couldn't wait much longer," chuckled Sarah's mother, Mrs. Andrews.

Her companion walked over to where Julie was still studying the map. "Are you the navigator?"

Julie looked up with a grin. "Oh, hi, Mrs. Preston." She was glad Marilla's mother had decided to come on the trip as another chaperone. She was fun. "I'm just trying to figure out where we are and how much further we have to go. Mike told me if I asked him again I was going to have to walk."

"Hmm," Mrs. Preston mused. "I'll have to try that technique. My crew is about to drive me crazy. I've been wishing I could give them something that would knock them out until we get there."

• • •

Julie was silent as they crossed the waterways leading from Fort Myers to Sanibel Island. She didn't think she had ever seen anything so beautiful. The wind was kicking up white caps in the Gulf of Mexico and on the bay side of the bridge, but the deep blue of the water was still dazzling. Tall palm trees, looking like feather dusters upside down, lined the road and swayed gently in the breeze. As they crossed the bridges leading to the island, graceful brown pelicans and white seagulls kept pace with their car, dipping and swirling in the air. They passed one beach dotted with several dozen windsurfers. The bright colors of their boards and sails flashing across the water reminded Julie of colorful birds skimming across the ocean. The best part was the warm balminess of the air. Mike and Coach had opened their windows and the van was filled with a salty, warm ocean breeze.

Julie lay back against her seat with a sigh. This was going to be paradise! She could feel herself relaxing already. She leaned forward again, eager to not miss anything, as they turned onto the island and wound their way down the main road under tall live oak trees draped with gently swaying Spanish moss. Bicyclists were everywhere on the bike path lining the left side of the road. Coach Crompton had told them Sanibel Island was a very exclusive and private place. There were stores and restaurants, but a spirit of elegance filled the area. The only fast food restaurant Julie saw was a Dairy Queen perched on one side of the road.

Julie's excitement grew as they turned down the road leading to their condominium. The trip had been expensive, and Julie had to promise her parents she would work this summer to pay back half of it, but she was already sure it was going to be worth it.

"Come on, Julie. Let's go claim our room!"

Julie had been looking around so eagerly she wasn't even aware the van had pulled to a stop. Grabbing her bag, she leaped after Jennifer. Minutes later she was standing on a balcony, complete with lush plants, looking out over the Gulf of Mexico. A sliding glass window stood open behind her. She hadn't bothered to unpack anything. She had thrown her things on the bed and headed straight for the balcony.

"Incredible!" Julie couldn't think of another word to express what she was feeling.

Jennifer was standing close beside her. "You can say that again! This place is really something. This is the first time the team has come to Sanibel Island. Come on, let's go check out where everyone else is."

Coach Crompton had rented two condominiums right next to each other. Julie, Jennifer, and four of the other girls shared one with their coach and her husband. The remaining five girls were with Mrs. Andrews and Mrs. Preston. All of the cooking, except for breakfast, would be done in Julie's unit. She thought the set up was perfect. The next 30 minutes were spent inspecting the two units and unpacking their bags.

As Julie emptied her bag she listened to Carla and Sandy talking excitedly in the next room. She wasn't sure how she felt about them being in the same condominium. They had come to mean nothing but trouble to her, but on the other hand, there was Coach and Mike to keep an eye on them. Jewel and Amanda were welcome additions. The next five-and-a-half days should be a lot of fun.

"Come on, Julie. We have half an hour before the meeting Coach Crompton called. Let's go look around this place."

Julie followed her willingly. Everywhere was lush greenness. The condominiums were two-story, gleaming white adobe buildings. Flowers, huge red ones and brilliant yellow and white ones, bloomed everywhere. Rounding the corner they found an inviting blue pool surrounded by towering palm and live oak trees. White lounge chairs and tables covered with blue umbrellas dotted the poolside. Just over the wall surrounding the pool they could see waves crashing in from the Gulf. Julie took a deep breath of the refreshing air. Continuing on, they found six tennis courts, impeccably cared for with white benches at each one.

"I guess this is where we're going to play," Jennifer commented. "Nice courts."

Julie nodded and then looked at her watch. "Coach's meeting starts in five minutes. We'd better head back."

• • •

Coach Crompton's meeting had been short. "I know you don't want to listen to me talk, but I wanted to go over the rules one more time. Mike, Mrs. Preston, Mrs. Andrews, and I are not here as your policemen, or women. But we are here to keep an eye on things. Your curfew is 11 o'clock. There is to be no smoking, no alcohol, and someone needs to know where you are if you go somewhere. Is all that clear?"

Julie looked around as everyone nodded their heads. She was especially watching Carla and Sandy. They dutifully nodded along with the rest, but Julie saw them exchange playful winks. What were they up to? Julie was thankful for the rules. She was just here to have a good time. She didn't want to battle the drinking issue. She wanted to play and she wanted to think about everything Martin had said the other night.

"Okay," Coach Crompton continued. "The rest of the day is free. I don't expect anyone to play tennis after driving all night and trying to sleep in the van. I want everyone to stay around here, but you can either go to the pool, hit the beach, play tennis if you're crazy, or crash and get some sleep."

"Now that would be crazy," quipped Jennifer. "I sure didn't come to Florida to sleep!"

● ● ●

Julie walked out on the tennis courts the next morning refreshed and rested. She and Jennifer had joined the rest of the team on the beach yesterday. They had spent the whole afternoon laying in the sun or playing in the ocean. The Gulf didn't have large waves, but the water was warm and felt like silk as it wrapped around Julie's body. She had hardly been able to keep her eyes open after dinner last night. She had been sound asleep by 9 o'clock. She already felt better than she had in weeks. Coming to Florida had been just the thing for her. It felt great to play outside under a beaming sun with fresh ocean breezes.

Julie knew she played good tennis that morning. She was relaxed and confident and everything seemed to work. She felt ready to take on even Sandy if she wanted to play. After three hours of play and drill, Coach called them over.

"Good job, team. I'm pleased with how all of you are playing. There is something in this air that is good for you. You've got about 40 minutes to take showers before lunch. Make sure you check the work list to see if it's your turn to help with the meal. After lunch you're on your own. Mrs. Preston and Mrs. Andrews are going to be taking a group over to the Ding Darling Wildlife Preserve here on the island to go canoeing if you want to go."

Julie looked at Jennifer expectantly.

Jennifer nodded. "Sounds like fun to me. I'm not a great canoeist, but it's probably a great way to see everything."

Julie agreed. "The worst that can happen is if we tip the canoe. The water is so warm it won't make any difference."

• • •

"Everyone needs to have their life jackets on while they're in the boat. You'll be quite a way from the dock area so if you fall in we won't see you and we won't be able to help. Are there any more questions?"

Brad, the canoe operator, had spent the last 20 minutes demonstrating how to hold the paddle, the different strokes, and how to turn the canoe back over if it flipped. He had told them the safety rules and showed them the route on a map.

Julie spoke for the group. "We're ready to go!"

Brad chuckled. "Okay, well then, go for it."

Julie and Jennifer jumped forward, dragged their canoe in the water, and carefully climbed in, steadying it for each other. Jewel and Amanda were in one of the other canoes and Laura and Amy occupied another, followed by the two mothers.

Digging deep, Julie and Jennifer pulled out in the lead. They paddled steadily for 15 minutes as they crossed the bay and headed for a channel through one of the island areas. They looked around in delight as a flock of large pink birds swooped low over their heads and dark cormorants dove deep into the water, bobbing up sometimes 100 feet away seconds later. Julie was amazed at the speed the cormorants could swim underwater. Looking down she caught the silver flash of fish as a school swarmed by.

Soon they left behind the brightness of the tropical sun and found themselves enveloped in the shadowy depths of a great mangrove forest. Brad had explained that the mangroves formed their own islands. The massive, tangled root system of the trees captured and held the silt and sand of the ocean, eventually forming their own land mass. Tiny crabs were everywhere as they scuttled along the branches of the trees, making plopping sounds as they dropped into the water. Bird sounds filled the air. White herons were as common as the robins Julie was used to seeing back home.

By unspoken assent, silence pervaded the group. They didn't want to talk. They just wanted to absorb the beauty and peace of the place. The whole group concentrated on dipping their paddles as smoothly and silently as possible.

Julie tried to look everywhere at once. She didn't know the names of the birds, but the bright colors as they flitted through the trees amazed her.

"Julie!"

Julie jerked her head around at the sound of Jennifer's panicked whisper. Her eyes widened as she followed the direction of her friend's pointing hand. A massive alligator slithered down the river-bank. Julie had never seen one in real life . . . only in books. She froze, her paddle hanging in mid air. What in the world should she do?

Just then Sarah's and Marilla's moms paddled up behind them. They spoke reassuredly. "Relax, girls. He doesn't mean any harm. He's just getting in the water so he can hide from you. As long as you don't threaten him, he won't do anything."

Julie heaved a sigh of relief. She certainly didn't mean to threaten him. She had no desire to tangle with a Florida alligator. Then she tingled with excitement. Would she ever have stories to tell when she got home!

The group paddled through the mangrove forests for almost three hours before they reluctantly turned back. It would take them at least 40 minutes to circle back around, and their time limit was four hours. Julie was entranced with the tropical mystique, but her arms and shoulders were beginning to ache. This paddling was hard work.

"How was it girls?" Brad asked.

"Awesome!" Jennifer's one word seemed to say it all. The other girls just nodded with shining eyes.

• • •

"I have a special surprise for you girls today," Coach Crompton said with a smile. "We're going to the Bubble Room."

The team looked at her questioningly.

"The Bubble Room?" Jewel asked. "What's that? It sounds like some kind of soap and bathroom stuff store."

All of the adults simply laughed.

Mike spoke for them. "I think you'll be surprised. It most definitely is not a soap shop. It's where we're going for lunch. Do me a favor. Take your showers fast. I'm starving!"

It took them about 20 minutes to drive across Sanibel Island to neighboring Captiva Island. Captiva was a narrow strip of land with gorgeous homes set way off the one main road that followed the pounding surf. Turning inland to a slightly wider area, they were soon pulling into the restaurant parking lot.

Julie and her teammates climbed out and looked around. It didn't look like that big of a deal. In fact, it looked a little strange, Julie thought. The building was a large, almost ramshackle building painted pink, green, and yellow with wooden cornices decorating the windows and roof overhangs. Julie and Jennifer looked at one another and shrugged as they walked in. Once inside all they could do was stare in wonder. Was it a Christmas shop? A toy shop? A collection of antique memorabilia? Upon closer inspection they decided it was all of that, as well as being a restaurant.

Toy trains chugged their way around tracks circling the ceiling. Christmas lights, the old fashioned bubbling kind that looked like candles, were everywhere. Pictures of old movie stars and singers cluttered the walls. The tables were glass covered boxes full of baseball cards, old toys, pictures and other treasures from years before they were born. There was a tiny alcove as they climbed the stairs to the upper level that was a Christmas bear scene with animated bears and figurines. Julie's head turned constantly as she tried to take it all in.

"Wow! This is some place," Carla commented.

Even she was impressed with the restaurant.

They found a large table already set to accommodate the 15 of them. Settling down, they opened the menus laid at all their places.

"Hi! I'm Bob and I'm going to be your Bubble Scout for the day!"

Julie stared at the cute, smiling man in front of her. What had he said?

Sandy laughed as she challenged him. "You're our what?"

Bob laughed easily. "I'm your Bubble Scout! I'm here to serve your meal and generally make sure you have a good time."

Julie smiled as she stared at him. He was dressed in a khaki Boy Scout uniform covered with bizarre buttons and patches of all kinds. He wore a large outlandish hat also covered with buttons and patches. Looking around, she realized all the waiters were dressed that way. At least they didn't have the only weird one.

Bob continued. "The menu is quite extensive, but I'd like to recommend a few things to you. The Carolina Moons are our most popular appetizer. In fact, they're why I decided to work here. I loved them so much, I decided to work where I could get them free!" He continued on, rattling off the specials of the day and other highlights of the menu.

"Did anyone get all that?" Sandy asked as Bob walked away with a promise to be back soon to take their order.

The whole table laughed as they shook their

heads, but everyone was ready with an order when their Bubble Scout returned.

They all used the 30 minutes before their food came to wander through the restaurant and check out the displays and decorations. Seeing Bob approach their table with food, they all headed back quickly.

Julie looked with delight at the order of Carolina Moons she and Jennifer had decided to share. She took one bite and settled back with a smile of bliss. "I'm hooked. I don't need anything else."

Jennifer hummed agreement as she stuffed more into her mouth.

The basket of Carolina Moons was almost enough for a meal. The Bubble Room had sliced potatoes to make their own fried potato chips and then had smothered them in cheddar cheese with a large bowl of sour cream to dip them in. The whole table had taken Bob's suggestion of Carolina Moons as an appetizer. Silence fell on the group as they eagerly consumed them.

Julie settled back with a sigh. "That would almost be enough to satisfy me."

Bob spoke from behind her. "Don't get comfortable yet. You have a long way to go."

Julie groaned at the sight of the huge French Dip sandwich he set in front of her, but dug in willingly enough.

Twenty minutes later she was holding her stomach and groaning. "I'm stuffed. I can't eat another bite."

"You can say that again," muttered Jewel. "It's a good thing we played tennis this morning. I don't think I'll be moving again for a while!"

"All I want to do is go get a lounge chair and die beside the pool," Marilla agreed.

Just then Bob walked up with a huge tray and a smile to match it. "Dessert time!"

The whole group groaned and shook their heads. But the tempting array was too much. The hardest thing had been what to pick from the 12 desserts begging to be chosen.

Julie opted for the sinfully rich three-layer chocolate cake. Jennifer selected the equally thick red velvet cake. Marilla ordered the huge cheesecake covered with strawberries, while Jewel chose the frozen Snicker's ice cream pie.

When the desserts, bigger than any the girls had ever seen, arrived they just laughed. Where in the world were they going to put them? They already felt like they were going to explode. Twenty minutes later the team stumbled out of the restaurant and crawled slowly into the van.

"I think this is a conspiracy to make sure we don't cause our chaperones any trouble," Jennifer groaned.

Coach Crompton just laughed as she started up the van and pulled out of the parking lot. "I hadn't thought of it that way, but now that you mention it . . maybe we'll come here every day."

"Every day!" Julie exclaimed. "I think you'll have

to kiss your tennis team good-bye. We'll all gain 20 pounds before we leave and not be able to move!"

"All I have to say is, please drive carefully," begged Carla. "I'm so full, any sudden movement is probably going to jostle all that food right out of me."

"Ugh!" Coach Crompton said, wrinkling her nose in distaste. "You have my word of honor. No sudden movements."

Silence fell on the van as they all leaned back against the seats for the ride back.

• • •

Two hours later, after naps by the pool in the blazing sun, everyone was ready for some action. Just then Mike walked up.

"Let's go, gang. My wife said to make sure you were tired for tonight because she wanted to go to bed early. My job is to tire you out."

No one moved. Carla was the only one to speak. "What do you have in mind? Sprints along the beach, maybe?" He couldn't miss the sarcasm in her voice.

Mike was brightly cheerful. "No, Carla, but I'm sure it's not something you would be interested in." He paused as everyone looked up at him questioningly. "I'll let everyone tell you how the jet-skiing was."

"Jet-skiing!" The entire team spoke in unison as they jumped up. "Where?"

Carla jumped up along with the rest. "Hey, Mike, I was just kidding. Jet skiing sounds great!"

"I thought you would change your tune," he grinned. "Follow me. There is a stand about a quarter of a mile down the beach. They only have six of them, so we'll have to take turns. Actually they're wave runners, not jet skis."

"No problem!" they chorused as they fell in behind him.

Julie moved up to ask him, "What's the difference between jet-skiing and wave running?"

Mike shrugged. "I know jet-skiing is a lot more difficult. It takes more practice and a while to get the hang of it. Wave runners are just like a motorcycle on water. You climb on, crank back on the throttle, and fly! They're a blast. A friend of mine out in Oregon has one powerful enough to actually pull a water skier. I think you'll like them."

Like them was a huge understatement. Julie had a blast! Soon she was doing 360s in the water and laughing wildly as she bashed through and over waves, soaking herself from the spray of the water. She felt like she'd just gotten started when her 30 minutes was up. Sinking down on the sand she watched as Jennifer crawled onto the one she had just abandoned and took off. Julie couldn't remember when she had had so much fun. Florida was a great place.

FOURTEEN

Two-forty A.M. Julie groaned and tried to go back to sleep but the pressure on her bladder would not be ignored. Throwing back the covers, she rose and glanced down to where Jennifer was sleeping. The other side of the bed was still made. Julie looked around the room in concern. She knew Jennifer hadn't felt like going to bed last night when she did, but where had she slept? Peering through her door into the living room she realized there was no body on the sofa. Rubbing sleep from her eyes, she went in search of her friend.

She had gone just a few feet when Julie found her. Curled up in a chair on their private balcony, Jennifer was staring out at the ocean. Julie hesitated by the door and then quietly slid the glass door open and stepped out. Jennifer turned her head a little in response to the noise, but didn't say anything. Julie stood uncertainly for a few minutes, looking at the ocean and wondering what to do. An almost full moon had turned the inky night into a place of magic, catching the whitecaps of the waves as they crested and bringing them to life. Absorbing the beauty for a few moments she then walked over and sat down in the chair next to her friend. Something was definitely wrong.

"You can't sleep?" It was more of a statement than a question.

The only response was a slight shake of Jennifer's head.

"What's going on, Jennifer?"

This illicited a slight shrug.

Julie took a deep breath. What could she do if Jennifer wouldn't talk to her? They sat together in silence for a few minutes. The early morning still was broken by a slight sniffle. Julie looked sharply at her friend. Jennifer had kept her eyes down since she had found her on the porch. Was she not talking because she was crying and didn't want Julie to know? Julie's concern mounted. Had something happened after she went to bed? When she had claimed exhaustion and went to bed the girls in her house had been watching *Sister Act* on the VCR.

Slipping out of her chair, Julie sat on the floor next to Jennifer.

"Jenn? What's wrong? Did something happen tonight?"

Again there was a shake of the head.

Julie pressed harder. "Then what is it? Why are you crying? Please talk to me!"

Silence lingered for a few more minutes and then

Jennifer's tear-swollen voice broke the morning. "I don't want to go home."

Julie didn't know what to say. She knew from her one morning at the Pattersons' house that things weren't great.

"Our time down here has been so much fun. I don't ever want it to end. There's no fighting, no screaming, no telling me what a bunch of junk I am, no wishing I was never born!" Her voice ended in a sob and then she fell into Julie's arms.

Julie felt tears flood her own eyes as Jennifer sobbed. What could she do for her friend? What could she tell her? Uncertain, she just held her and stroked her hair. She wondered if she should go get Coach Crompton but she didn't want to move.

Finally the tears began to abate. Jennifer took several deep gulps of breath and wiped her eyes with her pajama sleeves. "I need some tissues," she sniffed.

By the time Julie returned with the box of tissues, Jennifer seemed to be more under control.

"I'm sorry I lost control," she said in a tired, muffled voice.

"That's okay," Julie said. "I'm just sorry you're hurting." She remembered the things Martin had said when Brent was going through his hard time, and she had wanted to help. She knew she just needed to ask questions and let Jennifer talk. "Are things at home really that bad?"

Jennifer blew her nose several times and then

took a deep breath to steady her voice. "I've been miserable at home for a long time. It's gotten worse since I was 12. I guess I was easier to control and manipulate when I was younger. My parents aren't thrilled with the fact that I'm growing up. Actually they're not thrilled that I'm even here . . ."

Her voice trailed off. Julie waited quietly.

Jennifer stared out at the sea and then continued, "I'm a twin. At least, I'm supposed to be. My sister died in delivery. My birth was really difficult, but the doctor waited too long to do a Caesarean delivery. I don't understand it all, but somehow my sister died while they were trying to deliver me. I made it. My mom has never forgiven me for killing my twin."

Julie was shocked. "How in the world could you be blamed for killing your sister? That's crazy!"

Jennifer shrugged. "It's just the way it is. I didn't understand it when I was little. All I knew was that mom and dad yelled at me all the time. I can remember times when I didn't act right . . . They would come into my room and tell me they wished my sister had lived instead of me. That I was nothing but trouble to them." Her voice trailed off to a whisper and then strengthened, "It didn't take too long to agree with them. I wished I had been the one to die. At least I wouldn't be yelled at all the time."

Julie squeezed her hand, at a loss for words.

"Anyway," Jennifer continued, "when I got older I started to get angry. I couldn't help the fact that I had lived and my sister had died. There was nothing I could do to change it. So now, I try to make my parents' life as miserable as they make mine. It's gotten pretty bad. All we do is yell and scream at each other." Her voice broke with a sob. "I just don't want to go home. I wish I could run away, but I don't have anywhere to go. What am I going to do?" Her voice faded as tears conquered her again.

Julie held her close and racked her brain for what to say. Tapes of ways she had helped friends in the past played through her mind, but they were all words about Jesus being able to help with your pain, about giving your life to Jesus and letting him help you walk through your problems so you weren't alone. She just couldn't say them because she didn't believe them anymore. She wanted to, but every time she tried all she could hear was Greg's voice describing Brent's attempt to kill himself. God hadn't helped him. Why should he help Jennifer?

Julie wanted to cry herself as she held Jennifer. She wanted to help, but she had no idea what to do.

Thirty minutes later, Jennifer seemed to have cried herself out. Raising her head, she managed a faint smile. "Sorry to put you through this."

Julie shook her head. "Don't apologize. I'm glad I can be here. I just wish I knew a way to fix it."

It was Jennifer's turn to shake her head. "There's no way to fix it. I just have to hang in there until I'm old enough to get out of the house. I'll make it. It's

just that tonight it seemed to be more than I could
handle. I'll be okay. I just needed to cry a while."
Standing, she moved toward the bedroom. "We'd
better get some sleep. Coach told me yesterday that
my playing had improved a lot. I don't want her to
have to take those words back."

Julie watched her disappear through the door and
then slowly followed her. She lay in bed wide
awake, long after Jennifer had drifted off to sleep.
She had to find some answers. Staring out the window next to her bed and watching the moonlight
play on the water, she breathed her first prayer in
months,

"God, if you're there and you want me, come get
me."

• • •

Julie fought off sleep when the alarm buzzed in
her ear. Fumbling, she reached over and hit the off
button. 5 A.M. Why in the world was her alarm
going off now ? She had just finally drifted off to
sleep around 4:30. Her body screamed in protest as
her mind tried to figure out the puzzle. In the other
rooms she heard faint sounds of movement. Then
she remembered. They were getting up early to go
shelling. Her first thought was to turn over and go
back to sleep. Her sleep-fogged brain battled over
her options. She wanted to sleep, but she also
wanted to go shelling. Shelling won out. She could
sleep at home in Kingsport.

Swinging the covers back she rolled over to see if Jennifer wanted to go along.

"Don't even ask. I'm not moving from this bed," Jennifer growled from where she was already watching Julie get up.

Julie shrugged and smiled. "That's fine. I just didn't want to leave you behind if you wanted to go."

Jennifer shook her head, turned over, pulled the covers up close to her body and was asleep again before Julie even reached the bathroom. It took Julie only minutes to throw on some shorts and a t-shirt, and grab a windbreaker out of her duffle bag. She probably wouldn't need it, but if the wind was blowing down by the water, it could get chilly.

Twenty minutes later, Julie was walking along the shore with Jewel, Amanda, Sarah, Carla, and Amy. The others had opted to go back to sleep when their alarms sounded. Julie was already glad she had made the decision to get up. It was still dark, yet the moon cast lingering flickers over the landscape. Stars twinkled above, but the far horizon, changing from inky black to a dusky blue, whispered that the sun would soon chase them away to make sure there was no competition for its brightness. The breeze blew softly, but Julie didn't need her jacket. She loved the feel of its silky softness caressing her skin. She took several deep breaths to drink in the beauty. She, too, was going to be sorry to leave Florida. She had fallen in love with it over the last few days.

"Wow! Look how far the tide is out."

Julie looked to where Amy was pointing. The tide was indeed all the way out. She could see the outlines of shells littering the beach. Eagerly she reached for her flashlight. Sanibel Island was famous for its shelling. Located offshore in the gulf, it acted as a natural barrier to shells seeking refuge on Florida shores. Especially in the winter when they were sent hurtling to land by storms, the island beaches became home to thousands of beautiful shells. There were some restrictions on how many shells you could take, but Julie thought they were very reasonable. She was out here to see what she could find.

"Look at this!" An excited yell came from Marilla. "It's a huge conch shell."

They all gathered around to admire her find, but soon broke away to look for their own.

Julie found herself walking along beside Carla. She had been kind of surprised Carla had gotten up so early to come out. Getting away from Kingsport had shown Julie a new side to her former enemy. When Carla didn't have people she felt like she needed to show off for or prove herself to, she was really very likeable. Like now. As they strolled along the white, sandy beaches, Carla chattered about all they had done that week and how much she was looking forward to bungee jumping that day.

Julie and she walked along for about 30 minutes,

oohing and aahing over the wonderful shells they were finding. Julie was thrilled with her collection. She had several conches, a couple of starfish, one sand dollar and many she had picked up just because of the glorious colors and shapes. She had no idea what they were called. She just liked them and that was enough for her. Suddenly she had a yearning to be alone.

Turning to Carla she said, "I'm going to veg out on the beach for a while. You go ahead."

Carla also had a bag she was filling up with shells. "Okay, Julie. I want to find enough to make a border around the mirror in my room at home. After seeing that one in the shell shop the other day, I really want to do that to mine. It's going to take a lot more."

"Good luck." Julie turned away from the lapping water and walked up the beach toward the woods lining the shore. Finding a large log laying in the sand, she sunk down next to it and faced the ocean. She watched silently as the moon slid down behind the covering of the horizon. The sky seemed to take its cue from the moon's wink good-bye. In just minutes the dusky, almost black blue was replaced with a golden, purple glow that seemed to shout the coming of another day. Puffy clouds picked up the colors and danced in celebration as the wind blew them about the sky. Julie watched in awe as God created another day.

As God created another day. She realized the direction of her thoughts. Did she believe that? Did she really believe God created this day? If she did, then that meant she believed in God.

Julie turned back to gaze at the sky. Now the dancing clouds were being reflected in the smooth swells of the Gulf. The early morning slate blue of the water was like a mirror sending back its message. Soon its color would change to a vibrant aqua as the sun lit the depths. Tiny waves gathered and then fell onto the white sandy shores as they began their climb back from low tide.

Julie looked down at her collection of shells. She turned their exquisite shapes over and over in her hands. She held the conch close to her ear to hear the familiar roar. She gazed at the sand dollar and thought of the little dove-shaped figurines residing inside. How had its delicate whiteness survived the pounding waves and winter storms? Then she fingered the rest of her treasures and took in their glorious colors and fragile strength.

Slowly she began to understand the truth that was shouting at her from all directions. None of this could be an accident. You couldn't explain the wonder of the sky, the miracle of sunsets and sunrises, with simple meteorological data. The vastness of the ocean with its teeming life, endless mysteries, and regular tides was not just a mistake. Evolution and the Big-Bang theory could not explain beautiful shells of a thousand varieties. It had all been created by a Creator.

Julie nodded and laid her head back against the

log just as the sun split the horizon, splintering the last of the fading dawn. Deep blues leapt up from the ocean floor to greet the day and dazzling white sands returned the greeting of the sun. Suddenly, Julie laughed. She believed! She believed in God. There was a God out there and he had made all this to be enjoyed and cherished. She would never again doubt his reality.

But what about Brent? Sure there is a God, but does he really care about our lives? Does he make a difference?

Julie flinched as the questions rose to taunt her. She thought about her question from the morning. "God if you're there and you want me, come get me" He had answered part of her prayer. He was there. She would wait to see if he would answer the rest. Did he want her? For now, she knew she believed in his existence. She was glad.

Julie remained still beside the log for another hour before her teammates called her. She was content just watching God at work as another day unfolded before her eyes.

• • •

Jennifer stared up at the tall platform with wide eyes, all the time shaking her head. "No way. I'm not doing it!" Turning to Julie she almost shrieked, "Are you crazy? Do you know how high that is? I'm afraid of heights! There is no way I'm doing this!"

Julie just laughed as she pulled her friend forward

in line. Her own eyes were shining as she looked up
at the huge white sign with large blue and red letters
reading BUNGEE JUMPING. She had always wanted to do this. When Coach Crompton had announced
their plans for Friday afternoon she had hardly been
able to believe it. She and Jennifer were first in line.

Looking around, Julie realized the whole place
was empty except for them. Evidently, most people
opted to do it at night. Julie was glad she would be
able to see everything from the platform during day-
light. She was almost dancing in her eagerness to go.

"I take it that you will be willing to go first?"
Jennifer asked. "There is no way I'm going to do
this until I've seen someone survive it. In real life,"
she added. "Not in some television program that
edits out the bad stuff."

Julie laughed again at her friend's response. Then
she heard another voice over her shoulder.

"What about it Julie? Are you willing to go first?"
It was Coach Crompton.

Julie nodded her head eagerly. "Can I, Coach?
I'm dying to do this!"

"Dying! Don't use that word dying when you
talk about this."

Coach joined Julie in laughing at Jennifer.

"You can go first, Julie. I figured when you left
the van running that's what you had in mind. Have
you ever bungeed before?"

Julie shook her head. "I've always wanted to but
I haven't been able to afford it. This is great!"

Coach Crompton smiled. "Sign your release right here. I've already signed it where I needed to. By the way, your parents do know you're doing this. I just asked them to keep it a secret. I wouldn't let you do this without their permission."

Jennifer's voice sounded again. "Great. My parents told you I could jump to my death? Well, I guess they figured it's a sure fire way to get rid of their unwanted daughter."

Jennifer laughed as she spoke, but Julie recognized the pain in her eyes and remembered their early morning conversation. She was closer to being able to help Jennifer. Would this God she now believed in show her the rest of her prayer?

Minutes later, Julie found herself being buckled and strapped into the harness necessary for the jump. She looked up at the platform eagerly. It didn't look that high. This was going to be a piece of cake.

Ten minutes later she wasn't so sure. The climb up the platform had been scarier than she thought. As she and Carla, who would jump after her, had circled up the flight of stairs she had felt her stomach knotting. Looking through the mesh wire, it had seemed she was climbing to the top of the world. Now that she was standing at the top, she was sure of it. She wanted to appreciate the beauty of the Gulf spread out before her, but she just couldn't release her fear enough to.

"Okay, here's what you need to do. By the way, my name is Bruce."

Julie tried to focus on what the operator was telling her. He could tell she was nervous.

"Hey, there's nothing to this," he grinned. "I'm going to have you walk out onto that platform there . . . ," he pointed.

Julie looked. "Platform? It looks more like a postage stamp. I'm supposed to stand out there on that thing?"

Bruce nodded and then leaned forward and snapped the bungee cable onto her harness. Tugging her harness, he triple-checked what the girl below had already double checked. "It's bigger than you think."

Julie nodded doubtfully.

"Once you're out there . . . . Oh yeah," he said, "I forgot to ask you whether you want to go forwards or backwards. Head first or feet first?"

"I have a choice?" Julie squeaked. When he nodded she asked, "Which do you think I should do?"

"Well, some people think backwards is easiest because you can't really see what you're doing. But you may never get to do this again. Aren't you girls from somewhere in North Carolina? A tennis team?"

"Yeah."

"My favorite way to do it is facing forward, head first. You just kind of dive off the platform. It's a real rush."

Julie stared at him, her mind working furiously. He was right. She might never get to do this again. Taking a deep breath, she said, "Okay, I'll do it your way."

"That a girl. You'll love it!"

Julie was beginning to have doubts but she kept them to herself. Her whole team was watching her. She couldn't chicken out.

"Back to where we were. When you get out on the platform I want you to just stand there. I'm going to count one-two-three. When I get to three you jump. Just spread your arms and dive forward like you're going off a diving board."

Julie nodded, trying to ignore the fear gripping her stomach, and moved out onto the little platform. Looking down, the world began to swirl. Reaching back behind her she grabbed the railing. She couldn't do this! The huge air cushion beneath the jump spot that had looked so secure when she was on the ground seemed to be miles away.

"You can do it, Julie."

Julie registered Carla's encouraging voice from what seemed a long distance. She was only four feet away. Get yourself together, she scolded herself. You've always wanted to do this. It's no big deal. Releasing her hold on the railing she stood free on the platform again.

"Good, Julie," Bruce encouraged. "I'm going to count to three and you jump."

Julie nodded.

"One . . . two . . . three."

Julie couldn't move. She wanted to cry with frustration. It had been her dream for years to do this. Now that she had the chance, she froze in fear. She turned to Bruce with tears beginning to burn her eyes. "I'm sorry!"

He shrugged with a smile on his face. "No problem. Not that many people go on the first count-down. Let's try it again."

"Okay," Julie said but then added quickly, "Let me have just a minute."

Turning she looked down on the world. She made herself think about what she was doing. She knew the facts. She knew the stretchy rope holding her was good for over 1,000 pounds. She knew it was designed to last for 2,000 jumps and was retired to make room for a new one after just 500. She knew the air mattress under her would catch her in case something went wrong. She knew hundreds of other people had done the same thing and had nothing but positive things to say. She wouldn't get hurt if she jumped. Why was it so hard? Why couldn't she just trust the rope would hold her? All it would take was a leap of faith.

A leap of faith! The words jumped from her mind and slapped her in the face. She knew all the facts about bungee jumping. She had seen other people do it. In her mind she knew it would be okay and that she would be really glad when she did it. It was convincing her heart that was the hard part.

Julie realized in a rush that her faith in Christ was the same way. She knew all the facts in her heart. She had been learning them since she was a small child. She had seen other people live a life for Christ that was rich and fulfilling. She knew other people had taken that leap of faith and they were full of praise for what it was like. So Brent had tried to kill himself. He hadn't, had he? Hadn't Greg gotten to him in time? And besides, Brent had made that decision himself. God had tried to help him, had tried to show him there was hope, but Brent wouldn't listen. He had exercised his free will and made his choice. He could have died, but instead he was alive and good things were happening for him.

Suddenly Julie realized what she had to do. She wasn't going to let her fears and hangups stop her from living life to the fullest. She wasn't going to let her fears rob her of the joy of living. She was going to step out in faith and trust that God would be there to hold her . . . no matter what.

Julie jumped.

• • •

"What was it like, Julie?"

Her teammates crowded around her, shaking her hand and congratulating her. She had no idea who had asked the question so she spoke to everyone.

"What a rush! You think you're going to crash and then the rope catches you and you go flying back up into the air for the ride of your life. All of y'all have to do it! All it takes is a leap of faith."

Only Julie knew what that really meant.

FIFTEEN

Julie was eager to get back to the condominium and talk to Jennifer. Finally she felt like she could share with her about the Lord. She wanted to help her friend. She knew a relationship with Christ would be the best thing for her. That would be the beginning of working out her problems.

Just as they walked into their unit and headed toward their room, Sandy and Carla strode in behind them.

"Good news, team! We have a night without our chaperones. They are headed out to dinner after I convinced them we would be fine on our own for the evening. I say we all head down to the beach to enjoy our last night!" Sandy's voice was triumphant.

Jennifer's face brightened. She had been down ever since they left the bungee jumping place. She hadn't been able to do it. She had climbed half way up the tower, but her fear had driven her back down.

Julie's heart had ached at the defeat she saw in her friend's eyes. She was glad Sandy's idea had cheered her friend up, but she was concerned about the gleam she had seen in Sandy's eyes. She had seen it before. They had gotten back late so there was just time to change clothes before the pizza they had ordered arrived. Bedlam reigned as the team relived their adventures of the week, especially the bungee jumping. At least Jennifer hadn't been the only one not to do it, Julie thought. Marilla and Jewel had also declined the offer. The three of them were in the corner trying to laugh off their defeat. Well, Julie thought, it's better than feeling horrible about themselves.

She wouldn't have felt so good if she could have seen inside Jennifer's head.

An hour later, they were all headed down to the beach. Julie thought they would probably just walk around and maybe venture in for a late night swim. She was enjoying the warmth of the breeze as they walked past the tennis courts and the pool, and then down the boardwalk onto the sand. The team all stayed together as Carla and Sandy led the way down the beach. They had walked for about 15 minutes and seemed to be entering the island's park area. Tall trees lined the beach, casting shadows as they walked.

Suddenly, Julie saw Sandy and Carla dart off into an opening in the woods. She heard laughing and high voices. She exchanged glances with Jennifer, remembering the gleam in Sandy's eyes earlier. It didn't take her long to realize some of the voices she was hearing were male. She knew it could only mean trouble.

It didn't take long for trouble to walk out of the woods. Two guys, both looking to be in their early 20s, strolled out of the woods carrying a large cooler between them. Two more carrying a similar cooler followed close behind. With a flourish they set the coolers down on the beach.

The tallest one spoke. "I hear you girls have been deprived of refreshment this week. We're here to help you in your time of distress." Opening the cooler he pulled out a six-pack of beer. Raising it high above his head, he grinned.

Julie groaned to herself. What was she going to do now? The rest of her team had a different reaction. They had watched the drama in silence, but when they realized what was going on they laughed and clapped.

Sandy stepped forward with a grin. "Our chaperones may have delayed our fun, but they're not about to stop it!" Grabbing the tall spokesman by the arm she pulled him next to her and kissed him on the cheek. "Eric is the name of our rescuer. I met him by the pool the other day. It took some fancy planning to pull this off, but he and his buddies did it." Pointing to the guys in order, she introduced them. "This is Brad, Charles, and Matthew. They're down on their Spring Break from Penn State. When they heard about our dilemma they offered to help out."

It was only minutes before the coolers had been opened and beer was being passed around. Julie knew her moment of truth had come. She had hoped she wouldn't have to make a stand so soon, but she knew she didn't want to drink anymore. That was over. If it meant she was an outcast on the team, so be it. She had made her choice.

"One's not enough! Give me two of those things!"

Julie watched as Jennifer grabbed two of the beers, popped the tops, and with one in each hand began to guzzle. The light from the moon reflecting off the can showed Julie the wild misery in her eyes. She knew she was helpless to stop her.

"Here you go, Julie. It's celebration time."

"No thanks, Carla."

Carla was still smiling as she looked at Julie. "Oh, don't worry about it. We're not going to get caught. And what if we do? They can't do anything but send us home and we're all leaving tomorrow anyway!" She laughed hysterically at her own humor.

Julie shook her head again. "No thanks."

This time Carla's eyes narrowed. "What's the deal, Julie? I thought we settled this a long time ago. Are you a member of the team or not?"

Julie took a deep breath. "Yes, I'm a member of the team. But I'm not going to drink with y'all anymore." There, she had said it.

Anger flashed in Carla's eyes. "Too good for us? Or just not cool enough to know how to have a good time?"

"Neither. I just don't want to drink anymore." Julie wanted to say more. She wanted to stop all of them from being so stupid. She wanted to grab the beers out of Jennifer's hands and pull her away. She knew beer wasn't going to solve her friend's problems. She knew she couldn't say anything. The beer was flowing and nothing was going to stop it.

"So," Carla sneered, "Are you going to run back and tell our precious chaperones?"

Julie shook her head and spoke quietly, "No, Carla." In fact, she was going to stay right there. She had to be there in case Jennifer needed her. She knew her friend was acting crazy because she was hurting so bad. Jennifer had saved her from a bad situation with Marshall. She had to help her if she could.

Just then Sandy grabbed Carla's arm and pulled her away. "Give it up, Carla. We all knew she was a deadbeat anyway. If she doesn't know how to have a good time, that's her problem. Don't let it spoil your fun."

Carla couldn't resist one more jab. "It's your precious religion isn't it? Having too much fun finally got to you, huh? Oh, don't think I don't know about God! I know too much about him. All he wants to do is ruin our fun and trap us with his silly rules. Well, I'm not going for it. Take your stupid religion and go somewhere else!" After throwing out the heated words, she allowed Sandy to pull her away.

Julie wouldn't pretend that the words didn't hurt. But they didn't have power to control her anymore. Retreating to a log on the beach, she sat down to wait. Watching Jennifer, she realized her friend was already on her fourth beer. She wasn't drinking to have fun. She was drinking to get drunk. Drinking to forget her pain.

She saw Jennifer look around, spot her, and head in her direction. Julie stood to meet her.

"Julie! Come join us. We're having a great time!" Jennifer peered around the beach. "What are you sitting over here all alone for? Come on!"

Grabbing Julie's hand she tried to pull her over to the group.

Julie looked at her friend closely. There was desperation, even in the slur of her words. Her eyes were already bloodshot and reflected the same misery. Julie's heart went out to her. She pulled her hand free and reached up to grab her friend's shoulders. "It won't work, Jenn. You can't drink your problems away. They'll be here when you wake up tomorrow. The only difference is that you'll have a sick headache and nausea to deal with, too. Let's go. Let's get out of here."

It was as if Jennifer hadn't even heard her. She threw back her head and laughed. "I'm having too much fun. You should have fun, too. Come on,

Julie." With those words she walked back over to the crowd, grabbed another beer out of the cooler, and tipped it back.

With a heavy heart, Julie sat down to watch. The rest of the team ignored her now. She knew most of the girls were really great . . . until they got alcohol in their systems. Then all they could think about was drinking more and more until they lost track of what they really were doing. Not all of them were drinking to get drunk, but they had all fallen into the herd mentality. They would do whatever it took to fit in.

Julie realized that had been her, only weeks before. As she watched the girls' silly behavior and heard their comments she cringed to think she had ever acted like that. No wonder her friends had been concerned. Suddenly she just wanted to talk to Kelly. She needed her friend's steady understanding. But she couldn't leave Jennifer. She was going to need help getting back. At the thought of going back she realized there was no way Coach Crompton was not going to find out. There was going to be all kinds of trouble. Julie groaned and dropped her head in her hands. What had she gotten herself into? She should have taken the warning in Sandy's eyes and talked Jennifer out of coming.

Julie sat that way for several minutes. Suddenly a male voice broke into her thoughts.

"Hey, we're running out here. These girls are better drinkers than I thought. I guess we'll have to go get more." He laughed as the team cheered drunkenly. Then Eric continued. "Come on, Charles. Let's go replenish the stash. And I think one of the girls should go with us to keep company." He looked around the circle and his eyes rested on Jennifer. "This one seems to be the best drinker, so I bet she'll be the best company. How about it, cutie? You want to come along with us?"

Jennifer walked up to him and slipped her arm through his. "I'm all yours, Eric. I'll do anything for the man who released this team from prison."

Julie groaned again as she saw Eric wink at Charles.

Reaching down, Eric took Jennifer's hand and began to walk toward the car. "We'll see, baby. I might just have to take you up on that."

Julie couldn't let Jennifer go alone. But she also knew she couldn't talk her friend out of going. Jumping up she ran over and got to the car just as they did. "I'm coming with you."

Eric stepped back and then looked at her. "Who are you?"

"My name is Julie. I'm Jennifer's friend. I'm going with you." Her voice was firm but her heart was racing. Please God. Make them let me come!

Eric looked as if he was going to refuse but changed his mind and shrugged his shoulders. "Suit yourself. I hope you have the same attitude as your friend. Charles here is going to need someone to be friendly with, too."

Julie shuddered, kept praying, and climbed into the back seat with Charles. She might be making a huge mistake but she didn't know what else to do. She couldn't let Jennifer go alone. There was no telling what would happen.

It didn't take long to realize what kind of danger she and Jennifer had gotten into. Eric was clearly drunk. Julie gasped as they drifted over the center line several times.

"Eric, you need to stop the car and let us out!"

Eric just laughed at Julie's words. "You wanted to join the party, babe. This is the party. But don't worry. I'm not drunk. Just feeling good. I've got everything under control."

Julie lapsed into silence, trying to figure out what she should do. Just then her problems intensified. She winced as Charles grabbed her shoulder and pulled her close. The stench of his beer breath made her want to gag. Instinctively she pulled back.

"Come on, baby. I just want to have a little fun. Don't be so uptight."

"Don't touch me!" Julie spat out the words and jerked back to the other side of the car.

Jennifer wasn't faring so well in the front seat. Eric was much taller and stronger than she. Even as drunk as Jennifer was, she realized she was into something she didn't want. Still, she was no match when Eric unbuckled her seatbelt and forced her over next to him. Her feeble struggles went unnoticed.

Julie gasped as she saw the headlights of a car heading straight for them. "Eric!"

Looking up he cursed and swung the wheel just in time to pull them back into their lane. He laughed again and then bent his head to try and kiss Jennifer.

Julie was terrified. She wanted to reach forward in defense of her friend but she was afraid any sudden movement would send Eric flying off the road or into the path of an oncoming car. Quickly she reached up and pulled her seatbelt into position. She had forgotten to put it on when she got in.

She watched as Jennifer fought to pull away from Eric. Helplessly she looked on as he bent his head to kiss her again. Julie saw the headlights sweep around the curve in front of them, but her yell had no affect this time. Bracing her feet she waited for the inevitable. Just before the collision, she shot a glance at the speedometer. Forty miles per hour. Well, her last thought was, people don't usually die at this speed.

Seconds later the two vehicles met head on. The peace of the tropical night was rent by the screeching of metal and the squealing of wheels. Julie screamed as her body slammed forward and she watched Jennifer catapult into the windshield.

Then all was quiet. Julie sat sobbing as she saw her friend's crumpled body lying on the seat where it had been thrown back by the impact of the windshield. Blood poured from her head and she appeared lifeless.

"My car! Look what happened to my car!" Eric muttered in a drunken voice as Julie scrambled to open her door.

It was jammed, but by slamming her shoulder and hip into it she was able to force it open. Running around the car she peered into the driver's seat of the blue pickup truck angled across the road. The older man driving it seemed dazed but he had been wearing his seatbelt and seemed more shaken up than hurt.

"I've called 911."

Julie nodded at the lady who had run up from a neighboring house. Her mind worked furiously. "Can you also call the Seashore Condominiums and ask for a message to be given to Coach Crompton in Unit 242? Please have her come here or to the hospital. We're a tennis team down here on a trip. She's the only person to tell."

The lady nodded and disappeared into the darkness. Julie wanted to collapse in tears, but she knew she couldn't allow herself that luxury now. Just then Eric drunkenly climbed out his window and began to walk around his car.

"My car. My beautiful new Mustang. Look at it now."

"Yeah. Look at it! It's all your fault. But your stupid car can be fixed. Look at my friend. Look at Jennifer! What have you done to her?!" Julie wanted to attack him but knew it wouldn't help. He just continued to walk around the car and grumble. Julie sprang back to the side of the car. A quick look in the back seat assured her Charles would be okay. There was a cut on his face, but he just seemed dazed . . . or too drunk to know what was going on.

Just then Julie heard the faint sound of a siren in the distance. She wanted to crawl in next to Jennifer and hold her, but she was afraid any movement might hurt her more.

"Do you want to lay down young lady?"

Julie shook her head violently as the gentle voice of an elderly man sounded over her shoulder. "I'm okay. It's my friend." Her voice was high and shrill. "Where is the ambulance? Why don't they get here?"

"They're on the way . . . uh, what's your name young lady?"

Julie was aware he was trying to calm her down. "Julie. My name is Julie. And that's Jennifer," she said, nodding toward the still form on the seat. "She's too young to die!" she wailed.

The man moved closer. "She's not dead. She's still breathing."

Julie looked closer. Relief filled her when she saw the movement of Jennifer's body.

Just then the siren wailed around the corner. Seconds later Julie was being pushed gently aside and a paramedic was climbing into the seat beside Jennifer. Julie watched breathlessly as he examined her friend.

Julie! What are you doing here?"

Julie didn't know where Coach Crompton had
come from. She was just glad to see her. Sobbing,
she collapsed into her arms. Coach let her cry for
several minutes and then pushed her gently back to
look into her face. Julie saw that Mike was talking
to one of the paramedics who was loading Jennifer
onto a stretcher.

"Julie, what happened? We were on our way back
from dinner, and stopped when we saw the ambulance. What's going on?"

Trying to choke back her tears, Julie spilled out
the whole sordid story. "They were all drunk," she
said at the end. "I came along to try and help
Jennifer. I didn't think this would happen." Sobs
threatened to engulf her again. "What if she dies?"
Then she collapsed into the coach's arms. She heard
voices over her head but was crying too hard to
know what was being said. She felt herself being led
over to a car, shoved gently inside, and then driven
down the road.

She knew this night would haunt her for the rest
of her life.

SIXTEEN

J ulie was nervous as she padded down the busy hospital corridor. Kelly reached down and squeezed her hand as they approached the room they were looking for.

"You sure you don't want me to come in?"

"No, I need to talk to her on my own. I'll be okay."

Kelly nodded and squeezed her hand again. "I'll be praying for you."

Julie smiled and nodded. "I know. Thanks." Taking a deep breath she walked toward room 456. She could hardly believe a whole week had gone by since that terrifying night in Florida. Jennifer had just been transferred up to the Kingsport Hospital. She was going to be okay, but she had suffered a severe concussion and some internal bleeding. The doctors had told Jennifer's mother that she could probably go home in a day or so, but they wanted to see how she handled the move before they released her. As soon as Julie heard Jennifer was there, she had headed for the hospital.

Tapping on the door lightly, she cracked open the door. It was swung open immediately by Jennifer's mother. "Hello, Julie," she smiled. "Come on in. I know Jennifer wants to see you."

Julie gazed at this woman who had caused Jennifer so much pain. How could she smile after what she had done to her daughter? "Hello, Mrs. Patterson," she managed.

Looking over her shoulder she saw Jennifer smiling at her. Rushing forward she took Jennifer's hand. Once she was there she didn't know what to say.

"I'll leave you girls alone for a while. I'm sure you have a lot to talk about."

Julie nodded as Mrs. Patterson slipped out the door. She heard her speak briefly to Kelly and then silence descended. Julie gazed at Jennifer. There was still a small bandage on her head and some bruises on her face, but she looked pretty good.

"These doctors did a pretty good job, huh?"

Julie nodded awkwardly. She wanted to say so much, but she didn't know where to start.

Jennifer broke the silence first. "Thank you," she said softly.

Julie shook her head. "I didn't do anything. I'm sorry. You shouldn't be here."

Jennifer smiled, "I'm here because of a stupid choice I made. Coach Crompton told my parents how you tried to stop me and then went along in the car to try and help. There was nothing you could have done. I was too drunk to have listened."

Tears filled Julie's eyes. "I'm just so sorry it happened. So sorry you got hurt."

"It could have been a lot worse. I'm thankful nothing more happened."

Silence fell as they considered what *could* have happened.

"Do you know what happened to Eric and Charles?"

Jennifer grimaced. "What a couple of jerks. Turned out Eric was driving on a suspended license for three DUI's last year. Both he and Charles are fine. They are being tried for reckless driving and endangerment of life. Their court date is next month. They spent two nights in jail and will probably have to go back. My parents are going down for the trial. They've been really great!"

Julie stared. "Your parents have been great?"

"Yeah! I guess almost losing me made them realize they were kind of glad I had been born after all. We've had a lot of talks the past few days. There is a lot of hurt to be gotten over and dealt with, but I'm feeling pretty good. When my mom walked in the hospital room the first day crying, I wanted to ask for her identification. I was sure it had to be an act. But I guess it's the real thing. Time will tell anyway."

Julie nodded. "I'm glad, Jennifer." She paused and then launched into the speech she had prepared since the night of the accident. "Jennifer, I owe you an apology."

"What for?"

"When we first met, I was going through a really tough time. You know about Brent's suicide attempt?"

Jennifer nodded, watching her closely.

"Well, it really threw me for a loop. I just couldn't seem to make sense out of anything. I didn't understand God . . . how he could allow something like that to happen. I was asking so many questions, but I didn't feel like I was getting any answers. Finally I just decided God must not care. Then I decided he didn't even exist. That's why he hadn't been able to help Brent. I was pretty messed up.

"Since I didn't believe in God anymore, I figured I could do whatever I wanted to with my life. I wanted to fit in on the team so I did whatever it took. I started drinking. I blew off my other friends, and I started making fun of Christianity. But that wasn't me and I just kept feeling worse and worse."

Julie took a deep breath and continued. She described the morning on the beach when she had met God on her own for the first time. "I looked at what God had created and knew I believed he existed. I still had a lot of questions, but I knew I believed. And it was a belief of my very own. I didn't believe just because it was something my parents told me, or because I was trying to impress my youth director. I believed because God had made himself real to me."

She looked closely at Jennifer. She was listening carefully. Julie went on to describe her bungee jumping experience. "I realized that all of us have to decide at some point if Jesus is going to be real in our lives. I wanted to be able to completely understand faith. Well, I can't. I've decided it's one of those mysteries that can't be fully understood. Like bungee jumping.

"I don't comprehend all the reasons a rope can stretch and support weight and provide so much fun. All I know is that it works. Faith is that way. I don't have to understand how it works. I just know that it does. I was willing to jump off that platform because I knew it had worked for so many other people. It's the same thing with my faith. I've seen it work for so many other people and I'm watching it work in my own life. I may struggle in the future, but I'll never again doubt God is real and that he works in people's lives. It's not always the way we think it should be, but that doesn't mean he's not at work."

The moment she had been building up to was here. "That's why I have to apologize to you. I saw you hurting and I wanted so much to help you. But the only thing I once thought would help . . . I didn't believe in any more. So I just stood by helplessly. Worse yet, I entered your world and started doing the same things you were doing to ignore your pain. I could have helped if I hadn't been so confused."

Jennifer responded, "Assuming I was willing to believe what you were telling me." It was the only thing she had said since Julie started.

"Yeah," Julie agreed. "But at least I would have told you. I would have given you a chance to believe."

"Do you really believe all this God stuff, Julie?"

"With all my heart."

"You really think he wants to have a personal relationship with us?"

Julie nodded. "You sound like you've heard this before."

Jennifer nodded. "Carla and I both used to go to church across town. Our folks went there so they made us go to the youth group. A couple of years ago we started asking questions. We just weren't sure about some of what we were hearing."

"Carla went to church and youth group?" Julie was astonished. She just couldn't picture it.

"Yeah. Carla really isn't the ogre you think she is. Just someone who is hurting a lot. Like I was. Anyway, we started asking questions to try and make sense of things. Both of us had asked Jesus into our hearts and done the personal relationship bit already. There were just so many things we didn't understand." Pain twisted Jennifer's mouth as she remembered. "We never got answers to any of our questions. We were told that if we were really Christians we wouldn't be having questions. The fact that we were showed we weren't really saved and must not have a relationship with God."

Julie gasped in disbelief. Martin's voice, encouraging them to ask questions, rose in her mind.

Jennifer continued. "Both Carla and I were hurt . . . and angry. We decided if that's what the church was like we didn't want to have anything to do with it. I was mad, but Carla took it even harder than I. She's been bitter ever since we left. When you made the tennis team, and then played well enough to take her place, that was really tough on her. She was angry at Christians in general, and she just looked for ways to attack you and make you feel small."

Julie nodded. "She did a good job."

"She knows. She feels bad about it, too. She left school and came to see me this morning. She feels awful about what happened. Sandy is still being her stupid self. I heard she's having a big party this weekend. Carla realizes we could have died in that car accident. She's been doing a lot of thinking."

"I'm glad." Julie waited a few moments and then added softly, "Jenn, I'd really like it if you would come try my youth group. I understand how you feel, but this is different. Our youth director thinks it's great to ask questions. He even encourages us to. I still have a lot of questions. But now I'm honestly looking for answers. We're not perfect," she laughed, "though by knowing me I'm sure you've figured that out!"

Jennifer giggled at her friend's pained expression.

"I think you're great, Julie. That wouldn't keep me from going." Then she got serious. "I have to admit I was disappointed at first. I was kind of glad you were a Christian. I was hoping you would give me a reason to take another look at Jesus. I had been hurt, but so much of me believed what I had heard and I knew I needed something. I wanted you to stand up to the team for what you believed in."

Julie grimaced. "Boy, did I ever blow it."

Jennifer nodded. "Maybe, but all of us make mistakes. And you've told me why, and I can understand that." She lapsed into silence and then smiled. "I'd like to try out your youth group. How about if I ask Carla, too?"

Julie nodded eagerly. "That would be great!"

"Okay, enough religion stuff. Tell me about the team."

"Well, everyone was pretty shaken up by what happened, but I think that's good. The night of the accident Coach went to the hospital with you, and Mike headed down to the beach. When he got to where the drinking was going on, someone had called and the police were already there. Since everyone but the guys were underage, the cops hauled them in and charged them with underage drinking and public rowdiness. All of that is still being worked out. Each girl has their own court date."

Jennifer nodded soberly. "I guess we're all learning the hard way."

"Yeah," Julie agreed. "I think it's going to turn

out okay, though. I think the team has realized that following Sandy and Carla's lead did nothing but make trouble. Most of them didn't really want to be drinking. They were just doing it to fit in. I think this has scared them into being who they really are. Sandy seems to be more defiant than ever, but all I can do is pray for her. I can't change her." A slight smile played around Julie's lips.

"What's the smile for?"

"Oh, just remembering something Kelly told me when I got home. She and the guys were really worried about me, and just wanted to do something to fix everything. They finally realized that trying to force me into changing would only make it worse. So they decided to back off, pray, and love me. I guess it worked," she laughed. "Anyway, that's what I'm going to do for Sandy. I'm going to be friendly and try not to get angry when she slams me for my Christianity. Maybe it will eventually make a difference."

"I hope so," Jennifer said softly. "Sandy has had a hard life. Her mother is an alcoholic and her father was in jail until a couple of years ago for dealing drugs."

Julie gasped, "I had no idea."

"She doesn't want anyone to know."

Julie remembered the scene at Sandy's house the first night and her surprise at the fact that her parents had bought the alcohol. Now she understood more.

"Poor Sandy."

"Yeah. But don't let her hear you say that. She's got a lot of pride."

Julie's head was spinning. Even as she stood there she was realizing that it was so easy to judge someone without knowing why they were the way they were. She was going to try harder not to do that. God had put her on the tennis team for a reason. She was going to try not to mess it up this time.

"How are things with Kelly, Brent, and Greg?"

Julie smiled. "They're great. Kelly was the first person I called when we got home on Sunday. She came straight over and we talked for hours. I had already confessed everything to my parents. They were hurt and disappointed, but they were wonderful about it. They knew the accident had taught me my lesson. They've called your mom every day to see how you're doing."

"I know."

"Anyway, back to my friends. I told Kelly everything that happened . . . we even cried together for a while. She's pretty special. So is Greg. He just hugged me and I knew everything was okay."

"What about Brent?"

Julie shrugged. "We had a long talk on Monday. I apologized for hurting him, and we talked about how his suicide attempt had messed me up. It was good to really get it all out. I don't know what will happen in the future, but for now we're just going to be friends. I have enough things to figure out without trying to have a boyfriend, too. We're still going to get together, though. The four of us are going horseback riding tonight since the weather is so great!"

Jennifer smiled. "I'm glad things are working out. I should be out of here in a day or so. I have to take it easy for a while since things inside were kinda knocked around and my head is still sensitive, but I'll be back to normal soon."

"What about the tennis team?"

"Coach Crompton called and said my spot was still there for me when I get better. I may only get to play a couple of matches at the end of the season, but that's better than nothing."

Julie nodded. "She's been great. She let everyone have it when she got home from the hospital the next morning. She should have, though. We lied to her, went behind her back, and then almost got you killed. Once she calmed down she's been great in talking to parents and just being there. I really like her."

"Yeah. She's terrific. She's really helped my parents a lot."

Reaching down suddenly, Julie gave Jennifer a big hug. When she pulled back there were tears in her friend's eyes.

"Thanks again, Julie."

They chatted for a few more minutes and then Julie joined Kelly in the hall. Her huge smile was all Kelly needed to know everything had gone well. Quickly they walked down the corridor into the warm spring sunshine.

• • •

Three hours later, the four friends sat on their horses under the huge oak tree out in the pasture. Julie was relaxed and happy. Spring was evident everywhere she looked. Buds were bursting at their seams. Some had already escaped their confines and bathed the trees in soft green. Daffodils and crocus splashed yellow color across the meadow, and a warm breeze carried the delicious fragrance of spring.

Even the horses felt it. All four of them had pranced lightly through the woods and then floated almost effortlessly across the pasture as they celebrated spring with a grand race. Crystal, of course, had won, but Greg, on Shandy, was calling for a rematch. The four friends had laughed and talked as they rode.

"You seem like a new person, Julie."

Julie looked over at Greg and smiled. Visions of the last two months floated through her head . . . the pain, the questions and confusion, the partying, the tennis matches, the accident, her new understanding of her relationship with Jesus.

She smiled wider, a smile that took in her three friends.

"Yeah. A lot has happened. I guess you could say I've had a change of heart."

About the Author

Ginny Williams grew up loving and working with horses. When she got older, she added a love for teenagers to the top of her list. She admits she goes through withdrawal when she doesn't have kids around her, not that that has happened much in her fifteen years of youth ministry.

Ginny lives on a large farm by the James River outside of Richmond, Virginia. When she's not writing or speaking to youth groups, she can be found using her degree in recreation. She loves to travel and play. She bikes, plays tennis, windsurfs, rides horses (of course!), plays softball—she'll do anything that's fun! She's planning a bike trip across the country, and she's waiting for her chance to skydive.

Capturing the Spirit
of the Next Generation . . .
The Class of 2000
by Ginny Williams

Second Chances

When her widowed father remarries, Kelly vows to never accept his new wife. Then the opportunity comes to work with horses at a summer camp, and Kelly jumps at the chance. Getting away for a couple of months seems to be the perfect solution. But how much longer can Kelly run away from the trouble at home . . . or the turmoil in her own heart?

A Matter of Trust

Living with a new parent is a lot harder than Kelly thought it would be. Tensions build when Kelly's dad goes on a business trip, leaving Peggy in charge. Kelly constantly finds herself saying and doing things she later regrets. Kelly likes her stepmom—she really does. So why is she having such a hard time getting along with her?

Lost-and-Found Friend

Brent has a lot going for him—good grades, athletic talent, a great girlfriend. But home is a different matter. Greg wants to help his friend, but Brent keeps putting him off. And lately Brent's moodiness and brooding silence have only been getting worse. Will Greg get through to Brent before he tries something desperate?

A Change of Heart

Julie had always thought her faith was strong—but lately she's been having doubts. Surprised and confused by her thoughts, she searches for answers in new friends and a new attitude. If God isn't real, she figures, does it matter how she acts? But how long can Julie avoid the pain in her heart? How long can she keep running from God?

Spring Fever

Everything had been going along fine for Greg and Kelly—until Robbie. There's something about him that Kelly can't resist. Unable to give up Greg, yet curious about the new guy, Kelly tries to have it all. But if Kelly cares so much for Greg, why is she willing to risk everything on a guy she hardly knows?

The Action Never Stops in
The Crista Chronicles
by Mark Littleton

Secrets of Moonlight Mountain

When an unexpected blizzard traps Crista on Moonlight Mountain with a young couple in need of a doctor, Crista must brave the storm and the dark to get her physician father. Will she make it in time?

Winter Thunder

A sudden change in Crista's new friend, Jeff, and the odd circumstances surrounding Mrs. Oldham's broken windows all point to Jeff as the culprit in the recent cabin break-ins. What is Jeff trying to hide? Will Crista be able to prove his innocence?

Robbers on Rock Road

When the clues fall into place regarding the true identity of the cabin-wreckers, Crista and her friends find themselves facing terrible danger! Can they stop the robbers on Rock Road before someone gets hurt?

Escape of the Grizzly

A grizzly is on the loose on Moonlight Mountain! Who will find the bear first—the sheriff's posse or the circus workers? Crista knows there isn't much time—the bear has to be found quickly. But where, and how?

Danger on Midnight Trail

Crista can't stand her cousin Sarah, who does *everything* better. When an overnight hike into the mountains turns into a nightmare, can Crista and Sarah put aside their differences to save Crista's dad and face the danger on Midnight Trail?

Friends No Matter What

Kayzee's welcome to Crista's town is less than friendly. Surprised and hurt by the prejudice of others, Crista vows to stand by Kayzee—no matter what. But their friendship is put to the test when Kayzee's brother becomes a suspect in a robbery. Can Crista keep her promise in her search for the truth?